In the
Night,
on
Lanvale
Street

JANE LESLIE CONLY

In the
Night,
on
Lanvale
Street

Henry Holt and Company
New York

Henry Holt and Company, LLC
Publishers since 1866
115 West 18th Street
New York, New York 10011
www.henryholt.com

Henry Holt is a registered trademark of Henry Holt and Company, LLC
Copyright © 2005 by Jane Leslie Conly
Published in Canada by H. B. Fenn and Company Ltd.

Library of Congress Cataloging-in-Publication Data
Conly, Jane Leslie.
In the night, on Lanvale Street / Jane Leslie Conly.—1st ed.
p.   cm.
Summary: While helping a stranger solve the murder of a
neighbor, thirteen-year-old Charlie and her younger brother
are endangered by what they learn about gangs and drugs in
the neighborhood.
ISBN-13: 978-0-8050-7464-2
ISBN-10: 0-8050-7464-3
[1. Gangs—Fiction.   2. Neighborhood—Fiction.   3. Brothers
and sisters—Fiction.   4. Mental illness—Fiction.   5. African
Americans—Fiction.]   I. Title.
PZ7.C761846In   2005
[Fic]—dc22   2004059666

First Edition—2005
Designed by Amy Manzo Toth
Printed in the United States of America on acid-free paper. ∞

1   3   5   7   9   10   8   6   4   2

To my agent,
Barney Karpfinger,
with thanks

In the
Night,
on
Lanvale
Street

One

"**H**urry up!"

Jerry ignores me. His legs, as thin as sticks, seem stuck in place on the concrete alley, and he's pointing down: "Charlie, be careful." A pair of tent caterpillars ripple forward across the pavement. My little brother thinks they're beautiful. Watching them, his face, behind the frames of his pale blue plastic glasses, glows like a lantern.

"We're late!" I prod him back to life. It's my job to deliver him to day care by nine o'clock. I notice that his sneakers are untied, their laces splayed out on the dirty cement. I swoop quickly and tie them. When I stand back up, someone else has appeared beside us silently, as if from nowhere. He's a tall man, dark-skinned, dressed in a crisp tan raincoat. "Do you remember me?" he asks. "I'm Jim Chalmers. I lived at Mr. Healy's."

3

We stand there staring at each other. Mr. Healy was our neighbor. After he died, the renters in his boardinghouse had drifted away, like clouds banished from a cold, clear sky.

"I came back," he adds, as if answering our silent question. His eyes are so bright they seem to glitter in his face. "You're Charlene and Jerry, right?"

"Charlie," I correct him. He's startled for a moment. Then he takes a small, black notebook from his pocket and jots something down. I'm pretty sure that it's my name.

"I'll be talking to you," he says softly.

"About what?" Jerry asks.

But I don't have time to listen to his answer. We were running late before we even left the house this morning. "We're rushing," I tell the man apologetically. I take Jerry's arm and pull him after me. He lets himself be dragged, craning his neck backward. He stares at the raincoat man until we round the corner and he can't see him anymore.

Two

We don't know who killed Mr. Healy. Some people think Jim knows. He's the man Jerry and I saw yesterday in the alley. We kids call him the raincoat man because he always wears that tan raincoat, no matter what the weather. I don't know where he came from, but we used to see him hurrying up and down the sidewalk looking for something. He spoke to me once before, in front of my house. He was wearing clean, dark slacks and a knit shirt with the raincoat on top. He asked, "Did you see that boy running away?"

"I didn't see anyone," I said.

"He was carrying a black box." His restless eyes bored into me and made me want to squirm. Then he shook his head as if he didn't know what to do, even though he was a grown-up, but maybe I did. "He stole it, I'm positive. And they'll think someone else took it. Maybe they'll think it was me."

"What was in it?" I'd asked.

"I'm not supposed to tell." He looked down at me with that same nervous expression. "I wish I could—in fact, I wish I had it now." His face was kind, but to my surprise it looked like there were tears in his eyes. He shook his head back and forth, back and forth before he turned away. "If I only had what was in that box," he murmured, "I could have saved us all."

= = = = = = = = = = = = = =

Mr. Healy lived next door to me on Lanvale Street, in a faded pink shingle house with a wide front porch and a big yard. He let out rooms: two on the second floor, one on the first, with a bathroom and a kitchen to share. They went for cheap, but it was hard to find people to take them anyway. When someone came, all the kids on our block—me and my brother, Jerry; Shannon and Junior; Marcus Wilson and his cousin Kyle—would watch that person move in. We'd see what brand of TV they had, what kind of stereo, how many chairs they'd brought for the kitchen table. Most of the people who lived there were single. Some had gotten a divorce; some lost their jobs in a factory and were having to work at Burger King or McDonald's. One man had AIDS. A few had come from other cities, thinking they'd find something more, a better life, in ours. "I get the hard-luck cases," Mr. Healy used to say. "All they got left is dreams."

He liked them anyway. He said he'd been through hard times, too: His wife had died from cancer; his son was transferred to a job in California. "Some people think that they're responsible for their own good luck. They haven't visited that place where something happens and no one's to blame but you're out there by your lonesome, floating on a rough sea in a little boat, hoping somebody will rescue you. Or if they can't save you, at least talk to you, so you don't feel so alone. I've been in that boat, Charlie." He'd smile at me, pull my hair a little, just to tease. He thought it was funny for a girl to be called Charlie. "Charlene's a beautiful name. Why, think of all the women who'd love to have it—women named Beulah and Maude and Clarabel."

"Not me," I'd say.

"Why not?"

"Because it's wussy."

"Wussy? You?" He'd laugh then, a deep laugh that shook his round stomach and made the light brown skin of his face break into hundreds of lines. "Like all the roads I've traveled," he'd say, when he talked about those lines. "Because a face is like a map. It shows where you've been, maybe even where you're going next."

"But you're not going anywhere, are you?" we'd ask. So many people in our neighborhood had moved away for better schools, bigger yards, or what they just called peace and quiet. The ones who stayed were mostly old or stubborn, folks who'd put down roots and had no intention of pulling them up again.

Mr. Healy'd laugh and shake his head. "I can't leave you and Junior and Marcus and Shannon, can I? You'd raise the devil without me around. And what about Jerry? Somebody's got to keep an eye on him."

= = = = = = = = = = = = = = = =

My brother and I are opposites. I like to know exactly how things work—what's inside and how the pieces fit together. I have bits of things all over my room: clocks, car parts, a toaster, an old electric heater, an old TV. When I get upset, I take something apart and put it together again. It calms me down to see that there's a reason for each piece and a place where it fits just right. I think life is like that, too: God has a plan for all of us, and even though the puzzle's not complete, eventually we'll find out where our own piece fits exactly right.

Jerry is a dreamer. Mostly he dreams of animals and cars. He keeps a list of every car on the block, with notes: standard or automatic shift, V-6 engine, Goodyear or Dunlop tires. When somebody new came to Mr. Healy's, the first thing Jerry asked was "Does he have a car?" Most of them didn't. They took the bus down on the corner or called a taxi, if they had the money. The raincoat man usually walked.

= = = = = = = = = = = = = = = =

Jerry knew the raincoat man a little, and he liked him. But he doesn't know what happened to Mr. Healy. Mom told me not to tell. Even though Jerry's seven, he still has nightmares. Shannon and I aren't allowed to watch scary shows on TV, because he'll dream of them and wake up crying. Dad and Mom have to sit with him, have to rock him even though his legs hang down so far they almost touch the floor. I'm used to waking up and hearing that rocker *squeak squeak squeak* in the next room. "What's wrong with Jerry?" I whisper. "Had a bad dream." Mom always says the same thing. "Go back to bed, sugar, and I'll check on you once he's asleep."

He's a big baby. The other kids can make him cry just by stepping on bugs or throwing rocks at stray cats. Jerry tries—he puts on a face like he doesn't care. But they know he does. All they have to do is keep it up a little while, and that mask will start to crack. "Please don't," he'll say, trying to keep his voice even. "Please don't hurt that cat."

"She don't belong to you—don't belong to nobody. My old man told me to run her off. She peed under our porch, and my mom had to use half a bottle of Lysol to drown the stink. I'm only doing what they told me to."

"Please don't." Jerry tries to hold the boy's arm. It might be Kyle or Jay-Jay or just about anyone from our block or the next few down. It doesn't matter if they're black or white; when they see they can torment someone, they just can't pass it up. *Ping* goes the rock. Half the time they miss, 'cause those cats are fast. I see tears sprout in Jerry's eyes. "If you do it again," I'll tell whoever it is, "I'll turn Bobo loose."

"I ain't afraid of Bobo." But Bobo's a big dog. The kid's arm will go down, and he'll amble off like the whole thing is nothing, like we're nothing, too. "Screw him," I tell Jerry; but he looks at me so sad, with his shoulders sloped and his bottom lip trembling, that I feel bad for him. "Go look at cars," I say.

"I saw a Jaguar yesterday."

"Who was driving?"

He shrugs, still caught up in the gleam of it. "Boys . . ."

Dealers, maybe. They hang down on the corner of Lanvale and Belair Boulevard. Neighborhood boys stand with them, too, laughing and teasing when a pretty girl walks by. Lately they've noticed Shannon Johnson, my best friend. She frowns and rolls her eyes at them when we go past. You'd think that they were just a bunch of ordinary kids, except for the cars that pull up to the curb. I guess there's a signal, because a boy comes running from the alley, the car window rolls down, and something small is tossed inside. Money's passed over. The hands that reach out through the windows are black or white, old or young, and the cars can be SUVs or vans or Volvos. The drivers pull away and don't look back.

They didn't used to be here. Shan and I have tried, but we can't remember when they started showing up; because inside the neighborhood itself, nothing really changed. My parents called the police, just like a lot of grown-ups did. They'd come, three or four cars strong, and drive the dealers off. Yet as the weeks passed, they'd drift back, as if that corner had a power they couldn't shake off. We weren't supposed to talk to them or look their way. But over time we got used to their presence: something bad, but nothing to do with us and who we were—until the day that Mr. Healy was found dead.

He was dressed in blue pajamas and his plaid bathrobe, the same clothes he wore every morning as he sat in his rocking chair on the front porch, drinking coffee and reading the newspaper. But that morning he was lying facedown by the chair. Ms. Essie thought maybe he'd fallen, and she hurried up the steps to help him. There was blood on the porch floor, and when she turned him over, she realized he'd been shot.

We don't know who did it. But sometimes after I've said my prayers and fallen asleep in my bed, I dream I hear him talking. "Charlie," he says in his old, soft voice, "are you there?"

"I'm here, Mr. Healy."

I'm afraid, but I can't call Mom or Dad, 'cause Jerry might wake up. If I try to tell Shannon, she puts a pillow over her head, 'cause she doesn't like to talk about Mr. Healy. She says remembering him makes her sad.

"Charlie," he whispers.

I'm afraid. In the dark night, I feel like I'm at sea, in that little boat Mr. Healy used to talk about. That's why I'm writing this down. If you're listening, I hope you'll listen close. I'm not making any of it up.

He whispers in my ear, "Watch out."

Three

"**W**ake up." Mom's voice is like a wedge prying its way into my dreams. I turn over in bed, hoping she'll go away. But her hand lands on my shoulder, gives it a shake. "Charlie, I'm not leaving this house until you raise your head and look at me."

"Mom, why? It's summer."

"You know why. You've got to get Jerry to Mrs. Brill's by nine o'clock. She likes to have the group together when they start their walk."

Mrs. Brill is Jerry's day-care lady. Every day she takes him and five other little twerps on a walk around the neighborhood. You'd think they were on a guided tour, the way she stops and points things out. "Look, children, Mrs. Williams's roses have bloomed today, just for us. Does anyone know what color these roses are?"

"Pink," one of them shouts.

"Yes, Maya, good for you. They're pink. How many pink roses are there? Let's count together . . . one, two, three . . ."

They're into it, too. I've heard Jerry's voice along with the others, even though he's shy. Later I ask him, "Why do you go on those stupid walks? Don't you feel like an idiot?"

= = = = = = = = = = = = = =

"Charlie. . . ." Mom's getting impatient.

"Okay, I'm awake." I sit up in my bed until she goes away.

= = = = = = = = = = = = = =

Mom leaves the house at quarter to eight. She works for the city, answering phones for the Bureau of Public Works. She says her job's a way to earn a living, but she hopes I go to college so I have more choices. Dad works for GM, making vans. The money's good, but the plant shuts down if other factories go on strike or if they have more vans than they can sell. Then all the workers and their families have to hold their breath until it opens up again, because the company says our buildings are obsolete. They want to build new factories down in Mexico. Dad thinks it's only a matter of time until they do. I get excited when he says that: "Will we move there?" But the answer's always no.

My dad is short and muscular, with wire-rimmed glasses and a bushy gray mustache. He has what Ms. Essie calls a "closed mind"—it's already made up, no matter what you want to talk about. "My grandfather built this house himself," he tells me, when I ask him about Mexico. "His handprints are all over it. *Comprende?*"

But I don't. Why do grown-ups want things to stay the same? Sometimes I think I'd like to move to someplace new.

Shannon definitely would. In fact, she's got it figured out: Chicago. That's where her grandparents are and her favorite uncle, James. Her folks were raised there, too. They moved here, to Lanvale Street, because her dad got transferred by Citibank, where he's a manager. Her mom works for them, too, in accounting. Shannon and her older brother, Junior, go to private school. I go to Saint Mary's, six blocks over, because we're Catholic. We have to wear a uniform—skirt, white blouse, and ugly saddle shoes—and we go to Mass every morning. I complain, but the truth is I don't mind. I like the organ music, and I like hearing the same old stuff: *Thou shalt not steal; thou shalt not kill; thou shalt not bear false witness; love thy neighbor as thyself.* These rules make sense to me, and they don't change. It's good to have something to depend on, you know?

= = = = = = = = = = = = =

Jerry's voice is soft behind my bedroom door. "Isn't it time for me to go?"

"Uh-oh!" I look at the clock, spring out of bed, and run into the kitchen. I pour Jerry a bowl of Cheerios.

"Here, eat!"

"Can I have some orange juice, too?"

"Don't talk—eat." I pour the juice, run back to my room, pull on shorts, shirt, and sneakers. Jerry's clothes look like they're okay. But he's frowning:

"I'm not late, am I? I don't want to miss our constitutional."

"Your *what*?"

"Our constitutional—Mrs. Brill says that's another word for *walk*." He looks pleased and kind of excited. "We take a new route every day. Afterward we make a map of where we went and mark the treasures."

"Treasures?"

He doesn't notice the sarcasm. "Like if we see a kitten or a neat rock, or find a quarter on the ground . . ."

"Jerry?"

"What, Charlie?"

He looks up then, so trusting that I keep my mean thoughts to myself.

= = = = = = = = = = = = = =

Mrs. Brill lives on Abel Street, one block south and parallel to Lanvale. After I drop Jerry there, I come back home. Our house is stone, because my great-granddad, who came from Italy, was a stonemason. The other single homes on our block are shingled; the rest are brick duplexes. Beyond them Lanvale curves around until it intersects with Belair Boulevard. The traffic's heavy there: buses and cars racing for the suburbs, and dump trucks headed for the City Yard, three blocks south. Behind the yard there's a section where the railroad tracks go through. It's trashy and overgrown with weeds. When we're not supposed to be listening, grown-ups call it the morgue. We never go there. When I get to the corner, I turn north instead, and face the shopping strip.

= = = = = = = = = = = = = = =

Shannon works every morning in the Brite-Wash Laundromat. She tries to finish early, before it turns into a steambath. Right now she's folding clothes into a metal cart. She looks up and grins.

"You got rid of Jerry?"

"Yeah, he woke me just in time to get him to the grand tour."

"Thursday she's bringing them in here so they can see the wonders of the washers." She rolls her eyes. "I swear that woman's nuts."

"She's not the only one." We can't look at each other or we'll start laughing. Right on cue, the office door in the back flies open, and the owner, Nick Louras, comes strutting through. He's slim, with dark hair and light brown skin. His family came from Greece when he was young. He believes in business and most of all in his Laundromat, which is the center of his world. Whenever he locks the place or opens it, he says a prayer in Greek. Shan wishes he'd spend less time praying and more time sweeping, so she didn't have to. Shan doesn't hold much with religion. She thinks science can work miracles instead.

= = = = = = = = = = = = = = =

Now Mr. Louras asks, "How about those towels?"

"Almost done."

"Mr. Molloy brought in his whole month's wash—sheets, underwear, T-shirts, and socks." Mr. Louras sets the hamper on the table. "It's sort and fold."

"Who would pay to have their Jockey shorts folded?" I whisper. Shannon giggles.

"'Specially since he wears size 110." She holds up a pair, creamy white against her blue-black hands. "I bet we could both fit into these, Charlie."

We wait till Mr. Louras disappears into his office. I climb in first, sticking both legs through one leg hole. Then I drop the Jockeys to my knees so Shannon can fit in, too.

"You're so bony," she complains. "I'm not going to make it."

The waist is no problem—it's huge and it's elastic, too—but the leg hole has to stretch to hold both Shan's legs. One fits fine, but when she sticks the other in, something rips.

"Daag!" The leg hole's torn halfway across. Shan covers her mouth with both hands. She whispers, "What now?"

"We'll buy another pair, I guess."

"Where? Something tells me Dollar Discount isn't going to have this size." She turns the waistband over, checks the label. "Sixty-two!" She looks up at me. "Charlie, you got money?"

"Five dollars—think that's enough?"

"It ought to be. Go quick and come right back."

Dollar Discount is up the strip past McDonald's, Exxon, and Dunkin' Donuts. When I get there, they're just opening the doors. Out of habit I visit the birds and goldfish first. They have a canary I really like: She's almost always singing, even though she's in a cage with other birds. I named her Jess. When I asked Mom if I could have her, she said no. Jerry wants Jess, too. We're going to figure out a plan to get her anyway.

The Jockey shorts at Dollar Discount only go up to extra-extra large, which is a forty-eight-inch waist. I check Hanes and Fruit of the Loom, but neither kind is close to Mr. Molloy's size. I ask the gray-haired clerk, "What do you do if you need underwear bigger than these?"

She thinks I'm a pest, because I'm always in here looking at the birds. She says, all high and mighty, "I can't produce Jockey shorts that we don't have."

"Could you order it?"

"We don't special-order underwear."

I think of begging her, but her mouth's a straight line and her eyes say no.

= = = = = = = = = = = = = =

On my way back to the Laundromat, I ponder what to do. These times—when we're in trouble—I 'specially miss Mr. Healy, because if we kids had a problem, he was always ready to help.

Like the time we took Bobo off his chain so we could play with him, but then he bit the mailman's ankle. We'd been playing SPUD in Mr. Healy's yard—Shan, Junie, Jerry, Marcus, Kyle, and me—and we didn't notice Mr. Vargas coming up the sidewalk, or Bobo making a beeline for his leg. It was only a little nip, but you wouldn't have thought that from the way the mailman was hollering. He claimed he was going to call the dogcatcher and have him take Bobo to the pound right then and there. Kyle and Junie got upset and started cussing. Jerry was wailing, and Shannon and Marcus and I fell down on our knees and begged him not to. Then Kyle balled up his fists and said he'd kill anyone who came for Bobo. That was when Mr. Healy stepped in.

When he saw Mr. Vargas's ankle, he shook his head and gave my dog the evil eye. He said Bobo was such a terrible, awful creature that probably Mr. Vargas was doing the right thing to call the dogcatcher, that usually he didn't hold with killing kids' pets, but this case was extreme. When we heard that, we cried harder. Marcus said a prayer: "Jesus, please forgive this dog. It's not his fault, 'cause he's supposed to be tied up, but Charlie took him off the chain."

"Jesus wasn't the one got bit," Mr. Healy said.

Mr. Vargas looked uneasy.

"Mr. Mailman, we're so sorry." Marcus's in the drama club at school. Then Jerry joined in. He wasn't even acting. Tears were pouring down his cheeks like water from the gutter spouts.

"All right," Mr. Vargas said. "Would you please stop?"

"Yes, you children are creating a spectacle." Mr. Healy offered the mailman some Band-Aids or a glass of iced tea, but he said no, because he's got his pride. He's supposed to deliver the mail no matter what.

= = = = = = = = = = = = = =

Shannon doesn't want to waste time remembering the scrapes Mr. Healy got us out of. "Charlie, I have to save my job," she says.

"Did Mr. Louras count the underwear?"

"No, but I'm sure Mr. Molloy knows exactly how many pairs he put into the laundry bag."

We stare at each other for a minute. Then I say, "Why don't we write him a note saying we're sorry and that we'll get another pair? We can even ask where he buys them."

Doubt shows in Shannon's eyes. My schemes have landed her in trouble more than once. She thinks it over. "Okay," she says finally. "I guess it's better than nothing."

> *Dear Mr. Molloy,*
> *We are extremely sorry that we ripped one (1) pair of your jockey shorts. We will replace them as soon as we can.*
>
> > *Charlene and Shannon*
>
> *P.S. Could you please call and tell us where to get them as Dollar Discount does not carry a large enough size.*

We add phone numbers, then hide the note deep in the pile of freshly folded clothes. Shannon sticks her face into the sheets on top, just for a minute. "I love that smell," she says.

By then it's ten-thirty and she's off. Mr. Louras hands her a ten-dollar bill: "Good work." We head up the street toward McDonald's.

In summer, we come here almost every day. It's air-conditioned, which feels good after the Laundromat, and we're interested in the kids who work here—they're mostly juniors and seniors from Western High. They ignore us, because we're younger, but by listening from the booth around the corner, we learn who loves who, and where they went together. Shan writes down what they say in a notebook, even stuff like where they get their nails done or what they watch on TV. Now we order a Coke and fries to split and take them to the booth.

But we don't talk about the kids, because Shannon's worried about the underwear. Not only that, but her older brother Junior's been acting strange. She thinks he may have taken money from the stash she keeps hidden in her bureau drawer. She's saving because she wants to go to medical school and become a psychiatrist like her uncle James. She thinks the human mind's the next frontier.

"You know how they explored the Old West until they'd seen it all? Well, there's still tons that we don't know about the brain and what makes people think and act the way they do."

Sometimes Shan seems a lot more mature than me. I just want to go home and play Barbies on the front porch, like we used to. But we've been friends so long that she can read my mind.

"We're really too old for doll games. But we should do it once or twice, so all the Barbie clothes don't go to waste."

"They never talk about stuff like that, do they?"

She knows I mean the high school kids. She grins. "They probably have a trunk full of toys. They go home and play with them, and no one knows." Then she asks, out of the blue, "Do you remember the stories?"

Because we're such good friends, I don't even have to ask what she's talking about.

Four

Day care's over, and we're on our way to Uncle Mac's Exxon station—Jerry's favorite place. It's north of McDonald's on the boulevard. Uncle Mac isn't really our uncle; he's the old man who owns the station and lives behind it in a tiny beat-up house with a million stray cats. Jerry doesn't mind that the gas station office is filthy and the lot is filled with junky cars: a blue Dodge Dart, a Karmann Ghia convertible, a Ford Fairlane wagon, a gold and cream Buick LeSabre, and two Chevy Citations. (Dad says they're GM's worst mistakes.) Most of the cars have "As Is" written across the windshield. Two are propped on concrete blocks.

Uncle Mac's filling the tank on a bread truck. He's tall and thin, dressed in a pair of greasy coveralls. His eyes are blue, and his hair is dark gray, and he always looks like he forgot to shave. On summer evenings he and Mr. Healy played chess on the front porch. We got used to the way he'd tug down the brim of his dirty Orioles cap and say quietly, "Arthur, that's checkmate."

Now the driver of the bread truck gives him a crate of hamburger rolls. "They're day-old," Uncle Mac explains, handing us a couple packs, "so tell your mom to put them in the freezer."

Jerry knows who the other rolls are for. "Can I feed your cats?"

The old man nods toward an ancient refrigerator in one corner of the office. Jerry pulls out a gallon container of milk, then gathers aluminum pans from the office floor. He takes out some rolls, makes a layer in the bottom of the pans, pours the milk over. Cats appear like magic—from the garage, the bathroom, from the pavement by the used car lot.

"Baldy's in the Citation," Uncle Mac tells Jerry. "Don't let him out, 'cause he's been fighting with Harve."

Even before Jerry opens the Citation door, you can smell stink. The air inside the car's hot but not boiling, 'cause there's a box fan running in the side window. It's jammed in so that Baldy, who's gray-striped with a scarred head, can't escape. "Don't step on the extension cord," Jerry warns me. I'm holding my nose.

"There. . . ." Jerry sticks the pan in and slams the door.

A large orange cat springs for the opening, too late. He splats against the hot metal, growls angrily, shakes himself before he stalks off.

"You okay, Harve?" My brother hurries after him.

"He don't listen to no one," Uncle Mac mutters.

"What if he was in the car and Baldy stayed outside?"

"He'd rip the seat to shreds. Harve ain't got an ounce of self-restraint."

In the meantime a crowd of cats has gathered at the food pans. They're lapping and mewing; some are gobbling bread as if they haven't had a meal in weeks. Most of them have names: Brenda, Spotty, Brown Boy, Nancy, Carla. Then there's Pretty Girl, Queenie, Dog Face, Mushroom, China. There's a black cat I've never seen before and a gray tiger I don't recognize, either. Jerry says she lives in the convertible.

"How's he ever going to sell those cars, Jerry? They stink like cats."

"Some people like that smell."

"The two of you are nuts."

He's so happy feeding the cats that he doesn't bother to answer.

= = = = = = = = = = = = = =

Later we go past Dollar Discount. Jess is sitting on a perch by herself, above the parakeets. Her yellow outshines their pale blues and greens. They chitter away, but when she sees us, she raises her head and the feathers around her neck seem to swell. She sings. Her trilling takes me far away, to someplace green and lovely. When she's done, I have to blink my eyes. Jerry squeezes my hand. I forgot that I was holding his.

"We better go, huh, Charlie? Aren't we supposed to be back by four?"

We hurry down the sidewalk. Commuter traffic—cars on their way from downtown to the suburbs—swells the noise. We run up Lanvale, hoping to get home before Mom.

Five

When the front door opens, we pretend that we've been here for hours. Mom calls to us, then plops down on the couch, takes out her hairpins, and leans her head back, so that her curly red hair spreads out behind her like a pillow. She's pretty, despite some lines around her eyes and mouth. Dad found her serving sodas and peanuts to the crowd at the baseball game when she was just sixteen. When he asked her for matches, she refused him. *"I'm not going to help you kill yourself, buddy."*

"I'm not Buddy, I'm Dominic—Dom, for short. I'm leaving for the Persian Gulf a week from Sunday. I usually don't smoke, but I'm a little nervous. . . ."

"That makes sense, I guess. But what about when you get back?"

"I'll quit then, I promise—if you'll go out with me tonight. . . ."

That's how they got started, fourteen years ago. Mom says it's been forever. She's all worn out, so Jerry and I bring her soda or iced tea when she comes home. She grins when she sees us, slips her shoes off, and pats the couch on both sides of her so we'll sit down. "Charlie and Jerry-Boy," she usually says. "Tell me about your day."

= = = = = = = = = = = = = =

An hour later Dad comes in. He goes upstairs and takes a shower, "to get the dust off." Then he gets a beer from the refrigerator and sits down to watch the news. By then Jerry and I have set the table and dinner's almost ready. We've let Bobo in, and we're playing with him on the floor. Usually Dad just fusses at the news reporters, but now and then, if he's not too tired, he takes off his glasses, puts them on the dining room table, and gets down on the floor with us. "Who owns this great big ugly dog?" he asks.

"He's not ugly!" Jerry starts wrestling with Dad, and even though I'm thirteen, sometimes I join in, too. Bobo pretends to bare his teeth, but his tail is wagging. We roll around on the floor until we almost knock the fan over.

Mom's standing in the kitchen doorway, frowning, but her eyes are bright. She likes to see us having fun. "You all go clean up," she says. "Then we'll eat."

Dad says grace. Then we go over the day again. Jerry tells about day care and Uncle Mac's and seeing Jess at Dollar Discount. "She sang a song about wanting to live with us," he tells Mom. "I heard the words."

"Then you'd better sing your own song back and tell her no."

"Moooooom. . . ." Jerry and I won't give up, but she doesn't seem to budge. As usual, Dad sticks up for her. He's like a king. Jerry and I are the commoners.

"Charlie, don't argue with your mother."

"Why not?"

"Because I said so."

Mom says Dad and I are both so hardheaded, no wonder the sparks fly. I don't give up: "How come we can't discuss it?"

"Because your mother said no."

"I thought you believed in democracy. I thought that's what you fought for, in the war."

He gets upset if you mention that. Now he glowers. "Democracy is a form of government. Families are run by parents, 'cause they're older and they know what's best."

"If you know what's best, why don't we have more money? Then we could pay our bills and go to Hawaii, like the Shumachers did."

Jerry and I aren't supposed to talk back, even when we're obviously right. But Dad doesn't get the last word. Before he can say "Go to your room," I'm on my way upstairs.

= = = = = = = = = = = = = = =

I like my room. I've got a small TV and a Nintendo, my books, my tool set, and a double window that looks out on the street. I keep emergency supplies in my top dresser drawer. Now I get an apple and some little Milky Ways and lie down on my bed. Outside, Mr. Healy's pink house is glowing in the sunset.

= = = = = = = = = = = = = = =

I dreamed I heard his voice again on Sunday night. And yesterday—Monday—we saw Jim. They say that he was in the house when Mr. Healey died. Another boarder spent that night away; the third, Mrs. Bridges, slept through everything.

The police haven't figured out who did it. They interviewed all the boarders. The raincoat man thought he'd heard the bell around eleven, maybe even heard somebody talking, but he was in his own room, watching TV.

For a day or two, he was a suspect. But the police dropped that, 'cause he was so upset. They said he cried because Mr. Healy was the only one who'd offered him a place to live. Though he'd been there for months, he'd never finished unpacking. When the police searched his room, they found brand new T-shirts and socks, still in their wrappers. They found shoes so polished even the soles were clean. There was a Bible on the bedside table.

Mr. Healy had a Bible, too. Sometimes he read us psalms

he liked, or parables. The way he read them made the stories seem like they were happening now.

His son, Robert, flew in from California to administer the will. But it didn't say much: Robert got first pick of what was there. Uncle Mac got the box with the chess pieces, and the boarders could take any household goods. Ms. Essie, who'd sometimes listened to the ball game with Mr. Healy after supper, got the vase he'd bought in Singapore when he was a merchant seaman. Junior got his H & W auto parts cap. His beat-up car went to the Kidney Foundation. I didn't ask for anything. What he had didn't seem so special after he was dead.

His house is going to be sold, but that can't be done till certain papers are processed. Right now it's sitting empty. When I stand in front of it, the shingle walls seem like saggy pink cheeks and the two big windows on each side of the door look like eyes. Tonight, in the dusk, I imagine that they're crying.

= = = = = = = = = = = = = =

Later, the phone rings.

Mom and Dad and Jerry have walked to Baskin-Robbins for ice cream. I'm not supposed to answer it when they're not home, but I think it might be Shan, so I do it anyway.

"Is this Charlene?" somebody asks.

"Yeah. . . ."

"This is Edward Molloy."

I'm caught off guard. "Wh-wh-where can we buy your underwear?"

"I purchase my clothes at the Large and Tall Men's Shop, in Medlin. I'd like to have the underwear replaced within one week."

"Okay."

I write down his address, which is nearby.

"That's all then," he says briskly. "Good-bye."

∎ ∎ ∎ ∎ ∎ ∎ ∎ ∎ ∎ ∎ ∎ ∎ ∎ ∎ ∎

I call Shan right away. "What do you want?" she snaps. She's in the middle of the nighttime soaps.

"Mr. Molloy called." I tell her what he said, and about the store.

"I don't know which bus runs out there," Shan says doubtfully.

"The routes are marked on a map in the front of the phone book." Then I realize that I didn't tell her about seeing Jim.

"Jim was there when Mr. Healy died. I want to ask him about that night. He may remember things he didn't tell the police."

"What if he does? All the questions in the world—all the answers—won't bring Mr. Healy back."

"Until we find whoever did it, the rest of us could be in danger, too."

"Don't say *we*. This is one plan you're not about to hook me into."

"The person who killed my next-door neighbor is walking around scot-free!"

Shan sighs. Then she says, in her worst wiser-than-you tone, "Tomorrow, you and I are going to talk about this."

Six

Before we get a chance to talk, I see the raincoat man again. After I drop Jerry off, I turn the corner to cut through to the boulevard. He's standing in the middle of the alley. He looks as if he's been expecting me.

"Charlie," he says, "you came. Now you can help me find them."

"Who?"

He steps back, as if the answer is too obvious for words. Even in this heat, his raincoat's clean and pressed.

"The killers."

"You mean the ones who shot—"

He interrupts. "They're here, all right—all around, so you can't tell them from the rest." The whites of his eyes look big, as if he's terrified. "That's what makes it bad."

"But . . . are they crackheads? Or someone who broke in looking for money?"

"They'll get me if I say."

"Where are you living now?"

"I can't tell you. It's too dangerous. But I'll meet you here again. Then we can talk some more." He holds out his hand, and I shake it. His nails are neatly trimmed, and his palm feels dry and soft.

"The guilty must be confronted. That's where you and I come in—Jerry, too." He smiles then, like he knows Jerry's special. I smile back.

"Jerry doesn't know how Mr. Healy died. He thinks he had a heart attack or something."

"Yes, yes." Jim nods as if he understands. "I'll see you soon," he says.

I hurry to meet Shan.

= = = = = = = = = = = = = = =

She's got a pile of folding a mile high. Sweat is streaming down her face, and after a minute, it's streaming down mine, too. I help her fold, but we wait till we get to McDonald's to really talk. Once we have our Coke and fries, I tell Shan about this morning.

"He does know stuff about the murder," I explain. "But he's afraid to say, in case he gets hurt, too."

"Maybe they were friends of his. He could have let them in that night, not knowing what they planned to do."

"I don't think he had friends. Remember how he

hung around the porch and listened to the stories, just like us?"

"That doesn't mean he didn't have friends. They could have been from work, or a club, even a sports team." She sits thinking. A good-looking guy crosses the room to throw his trash away. Her eyes follow his every move. After he leaves, she turns back. "I think you should stay out of it. You could put yourself in danger, too."

Ms. Essie says that I'm the devil's advocate. "If we don't find the killer, who will? The police are used to injustice. They accept it."

She seems doubtful. But my words spill out like salt from the round blue box with the little girl and her umbrella.

"Whoever killed him could be sitting in this room right now."

She looks at me and doesn't answer.

= = = = = = = = = = = = = =

By the time I pick up Jerry, Mom's already home. She's giving me the evil eye for being late. I set the table without being asked.

We have a summer supper—sliced ham and potato salad and pickled beets. My folks are tired; they settle down to watch TV. Then Jerry and I take Bobo outside and sit on the front porch.

Nobody's out tonight. Last summer, on an evening like this, we kids would have been at Mr. Healy's. He told stories after he finished playing chess with Uncle Mac. They could be about anything: when he was a little boy in Florida, which was mostly cattle ranches back then; when he picked fruit in California and lived in the hobo camps; the jobs he had in the kitchens of fancy restaurants in New York City; the time he rode across the country on a Greyhound bus, and the lady in the next seat over had a baby somewhere in the middle of Ohio. "Tell about Chicago," Shannon used to beg. Then Mr. Healy would talk about Lake Michigan, and the el train, and the Loop, and the steak houses and pizza parlors and department stores. He'd even gone once to the ball game at Comiskey Park, where the White Sox play. When he finished, we'd beg him to tell more.

"Somebody else's turn," he'd say. "Let's hear from one of you."

But most of us had never been anywhere or seen anything. We were raised here in the city, had traveled to the suburbs in the county to see relatives, maybe taken the train on a school field trip to Washington or Philadelphia. Uncle Mac was from the city, too. He'd been raised poor and didn't like to talk about it. When Mr. Healy asked about those days, he'd make a gesture with one hand, as if the question were an object he could push away.

Seven

I get to the Laundromat just as the day-care kids arrive. They march in line behind Mrs. Brill and sit down in a circle of plastic chairs. Mr. Louras wears a suit and tie in their honor. He tells the children how his parents did the wash in Greece, where he came from, drawing buckets of water from a well. "The old ways had good parts, but lots of hard work, too," he says. "Now we have these wonderful machines."

The kids are excited. Each one clutches a dirty T-shirt. They've worked hard to mess them up: There's mud, Magic Marker, ketchup, and grease stains. The last shirt has a smear of tar on it. "Our normal stain removers won't work on this," Mr. Louras says. "But I have a weapon so powerful it even takes off tar." He douses the shirt with something green, throws it in with the rest, and turns on the washer.

After that they talk about water. What is it? Everybody

has an idea. One little kid says, "It's wet." "It's in raindrops," says Tanisha. They keep on talking. I wonder when Mrs. Brill's going to tell them the answer, but she never does. Then—finally—the wash is done, and the T-shirts come out. Shannon holds them up. Each kid yells: "That's mine!" They look to see if the stains came out.

Which they mostly did. This could be one of the seven wonders of the known universe. Shannon's into it, too, talking to each kid. They treat her like a star. Mrs. Brill makes it a big deal that she's got a *job*. Just before they start to wave good-bye, we snatch Jerry up, so we can go to Medlin. He's upset: "I'll miss *lunch*. Charlie, I love lunch."

"Jerry, you'll be there all summer."

His face screws up into a pout. I hate it when he gets like this. But Shan says quickly, "We're going on the bus!"

"Where?"

"To the suburbs. You can sit next to me, and I'll show you everything."

The bus stops at our corner, Lanvale and Belair. The Starcraft Bar and Lounge is just a few doors up the street. The usual gang is hanging out in front: Bitty and Jay and Kyle, who's from our block. He lives with our friend Marcus, but they're really different. When Kyle sees us now, he acts like we're invisible.

Mr. Tibby's at the intersection. He's older, and a Gulf War veteran, like my dad. He comes in the Laundromat each morning, selling newspapers. His hands and arms are fat from shooting up. Today his girlfriend Rhonda's by his side. She looks tired, but she's friendly anyway. "Where you girls going?"

"Medlin."

"So far?"

"We have to buy a pair of underwear," Shannon starts to explain. Rhonda stares at us.

"You're going all that way to buy a pair of underwear?"

The bus comes then, sparing us more questions.

= = = = = = = = = = = = = =

Jerry's glued to the bus window. He hasn't been on many trips, except downtown to the harbor on his birthday and now and then to see Aunt Ellen, Mom's sister, who lives in Fawn Grove, Pennsylvania. We go there in the car, so this is different. "What's that place?" Jerry asks. "Who're they?" We keep saying we don't know. We roll past brick ranch houses, their yards bright green and soft. Then the shopping strips begin. We pass the stores we have in town: McDonald's, Blockbuster, Dunkin' Donuts. There's a lot of car dealerships: Jerry's eyes bug out when he sees brand-new BMWs and Saabs. Finally the driver nods toward us: "This is Medlin, girls. Catch the bus home on the other side."

We wander through a giant mall. On the far end we find what we're looking for: Large and Tall Men's Shop. Shannon giggles as we step through the doorway, which is twice as wide as usual. I don't look at her, because if I do, we'll crack up. A scrawny clerk crabwalks over. "You girls sure you're in the right store? We don't allow no browsers here."

"We're looking for a pair of Jockey shorts, size sixty-two."

He glares as if he thinks it's all a joke, or maybe he guesses *he's* the joke, a skinny little bald man working in the Large and Tall. "Right over there." He points.

The problem is, they're in packs of two for $5.99. We breathe a sigh of relief when we see we've got enough money. We pay for the underwear and head on out.

"Too bad we can't get soda. . . ." Shannon's reading my mind. "Only the bus fare—"

"The bus fare!"

= = = = = = = = = = = = = =

We'll be okay if we pretend that Jerry's five, because five and under's free. We comb his hair forward instead of to the side, smear some dirt around his mouth. We show him how to walk with his knees bent and shoulders slumped. We stick his thumb in the corner of his mouth. He doesn't like that: "I hardly ever suck my thumb!"

Shannon teases, "You're supposed to say, 'I want Mommy.' "

"No way."

"How do you feel about walking home?"

He sighs resignedly, holds my hand when I make him.

= = = = = = = = = = = = = =

But the bus driver, who's a woman this time, knows better. "That ain't no five-year-old."

I look straight ahead. "He's big for his age."

"That boy ain't been five for a couple of years."

"He's five," Shannon says. "I was at his birthday party."

The driver stares at the plastic bag under Shan's arm. "I bet you spent all your money on junk, now you're trying to get home."

"This isn't junk—it's underwear!" Shannon shows her. The woman gasps when she sees the size.

"Oh, my heavens. I bet that did cost all your money. Go ahead, then." She nods toward the back of the bus, and we all ride free!

Eight

Shan stays home with Jerry while I run to Blockbuster to get a video. My choices are limited, because he can only watch films rated G. When Shan sees *Dumbo,* she refuses to sit through it.

"I've seen that stupid elephant a hundred times. . . . Come on in your room, Charlie. He can watch it by himself, and we can talk."

"About what?" Jerry's ears pick up on anything he's not supposed to know.

"Nothing. Watch your movie."

"I'll be lonely," Jerry whines.

"If you won't tell, I'll get Bobo. Then you can watch with him."

Bobo's so glad to see us he runs through the house jumping over furniture and skidding around corners like a racer. He knocks over a side table, flips a straight-backed chair. We put them back. "You guys are bad," Shannon says. But she loves Bobo, just like us.

We've had him since he was a pup: big brown head with a fat, wiggly brown and black body and a stumpy tail, which was always wagging, right from the moment he saw us. "Purebred," said the man selling him in front of Dollar Discount. Mom could see it wasn't true, but I guess she didn't care.

Mr. Healy liked Bobo, but he didn't love him. He thought maybe a dog that big ought to live in the country. Not only that, but when he was young, going across the west in boxcars and camping wherever he could find a patch of ground to lay his blankets on, he'd been chased by dogs. He had a long scar where a German shepherd sank its teeth into his leg. He got it when he was only fourteen, but you could see it plainly, a long pink line against the brown of his calf. "From that day on, I was a cat fan," he used to say. He and Uncle Mac liked to talk about cats. Mr. Healy would inquire into the health of every one of those strays, and Uncle Mac would answer like he was talking about his own family.

"Charlie, let's go." Dumbo's flapping his big ears across the TV screen, and Jerry and Bobo are curled up on the couch. We go upstairs and call Mr. Molloy. We get an answering machine: "You have reached the home of Edward Molloy and Tuyen Chao."

"That's his wife—she's Chinese," Shan whispers. Out loud she says, "We have your Jockey shorts. We'll drop them by your house in the next few days."

We hang around on my front porch. I'm about to get out the Barbies when Marcus comes by on his bike. He's the neighborhood busybody: everywhere, into everyone's business, all the time. When he sees us, he shouts, screeches across the yard, and slams on his brakes about an inch from the front steps. His big, round head, with its hair shaved close, reminds me of a pumpkin. He grins a toothy grin.

"Hey, ya'll—Ms. Essie's coming! She said she'll buy us ice cream."

"JERRY!"

He comes to the door, and I tell him what's going on. He turns off the VCR and shuts Bobo in his pen.

Ms. Essie is pretty cool, even though her glasses have those funny wings that make them look like they're about to fly right off her face. She's a retired teacher who lives four houses down. She's taught every grade but tenth, first in the segregated schools in Virginia but since then in the public ones here, too. She was Mr. Healy's friend; they'd sit together on the couch, watching the Discovery Channel. Sometimes they read books out loud, switching sides when they got tired. On Christmas, he gave her perfume, and she cooked a special meal for him and all the boarders. So it's especially sad that she was the one who found him dead.

= = = = = = = = = = = = = = = =

Now she comes strolling down the street. She's wearing a pale blue beret and a flowered dress. *Click click click* go her heels on the sidewalk.

"Shannon, Charlene, Jerry . . . may we expect the pleasure of your company?"

= = = = = = = = = = = = = = = =

Baskin-Robbins is busy. Once we get our ice cream, we sit together on the wooden bench out front. Marcus talks about his rec league baseball team; he's happy, because last night he hit a triple. We tell about our trip to Medlin. Ms. Essie cracks up. "I would have driven you," she tells us afterward. Later she talks to Shannon about Junie.

"He ought to have a job to keep him busy."

"He did have one, over at Popeyes on Layton, but the bus didn't come, so he was late, and then they fired him."

"Good as he is at math, there's no reason for him to be working at Popeyes. He could have an internship downtown."

Junie could beat both Mr. Healy and Uncle Mac at chess. He got a scholarship to go to private school, but I didn't know that he was good at math. Now Ms. Essie turns to Marcus. "Have you got your summer reading list?"

"Sheeesh, it ain't even July, Ms. Essie."

"It *isn't* July, Marcus. Anyway, you should get started, maybe get some extra credit before you lose points for talking in class."

"My behavior ain't that bad."

Marcus goes to Saint Mary's, too. It's true, he's far from the worst. I speak up for him: "He's not. They even let him be a safety patrol." Marcus beams.

She shakes her head in wonder, but she's smiling.

Nine

The next day the raincoat man is back. I'm on my way to pick up Jerry. When Jim sees me coming, he steps from foot to foot impatiently.

"Did you see anything?" he whispers.

"What do you mean?"

"Did they give themselves away? They make mistakes, you know—they're human, just like us."

I'm confused. "I don't know who I should be watching."

"Everyone."

"But . . . most people in the neighborhood are *good*. They wouldn't have hurt Mr. Healy."

"All but a few." His eyes bore into mine. "The world is two camps," he says then. "Good and evil. Being on guard is hard, but it's for the best."

"How do you know who's evil?"

"You watch for signs."

"What are the signs?"

"The devil manipulates. He'll put on the face of innocence to take you under his spell. Once he has you in his power, he can command your spirit."

"He'll take you under his spell." I say it softly. For some reason, I think of Jess in her cage, singing, and me listening, so wrapped up in the music I can hardly move.

"You go on now," the raincoat man says. His dark face shines, like there's a light somewhere behind his eyes. "Go and listen, and watch out. I'll meet you here tomorrow, and we'll talk more."

= = = = = = = = = = = = = =

I'm freaked out by what Jim said. If evil looks like good, how can we tell them apart? That night at supper, I ask my folks. My dad stops chewing in the middle of a forkful of ground beef. He swallows and peers at me over the tops of his glasses. "What have you been watching on TV?"

"Nothing . . . I mean, only the usual."

Jerry's staring. He mouths "Jim." I stare back, *shut up.*

"Good and evil aren't hard to tell apart," Dad says. "The Orioles are good, and the Yankees are evil."

I don't laugh. My mom notices. "Kindness is good, Charlie," she says. "Meanness and hurt are evil. Those don't seem the same to me."

"But Mr. Tibby's kind, and he's a drug addict."

"He's not evil—he's the victim of someone who is." Dad wants his say, too.

"What about people who kill stray cats and dogs at the pound?" Jerry asks.

"They're doing their job."

"But the Bible says Thou shalt not kill."

"Somebody killed this cow we're eating," Dad says, taking another bite of hamburger. Mom gives him a hard look. Jerry pushes his plate away. He's turned pale.

"It's all around us," he whispers.

"What?"

"Evil."

Dad growls, "Jerry, for heaven's sake, lighten up."

But Jerry can't, and I have an inkling that maybe Jim's been talking to him, too.

= = = = = = = = = = = = = =

After supper I go into his room. He's hunched over his little desk, writing something. He peers up at me through his blue glasses.

"I'm never eating meat again," he says. "Not ever."

I know then and there that he'll be a vegetarian for the rest of his life. But I can't keep myself from prodding. "What'll you eat?"

"Cheerios, applesauce . . . maybe spaghetti."

"You'll shrivel up and die."

Jerry shuts up then, and I'm sorry I tormented him. "You can eat macaroni and cheese," I tell him. "Oatmeal, too—the kind with maple sugar. There's no meat in that."

"Thanks, Charlie."

"Are you going to tell Mom?"

He nods. "Tomorrow."

"Jerry, have you been talking to Jim?"

"A little."

"What did he say to you?"

"He told me to be careful, 'cause evil's all around."

"He shouldn't scare a little kid like you."

"I don't think he meant to. Anyway, he was right."

"How come?"

"The hamburger we had tonight, Charlie—I didn't think!" He flings himself on his bed with his back to me and starts crying.

"Jerry, if you didn't know, you didn't do anything wrong."

"I didn't mean to, but I did."

I sit beside him, rub his back for a moment. What comes out of my mouth sounds lame, even to me. "It's going to be all right, Jerr, really it is."

Ten

I'm supernice to Jerry in the morning. The news about him being vegetarian has Mom rolling her eyes and on the warpath against Dad, who "should have known better" than to say what he did. Now she's pursing her lips as she checks the freezer for tonight's supper. She takes out a package of frozen chicken and puts it in the fridge to thaw. "Charlie, go by the Save-A-Lot and pick up six boxes of Kraft dinner, would you please? Here's money"—she hands me a couple of bills—"and warn Mrs. Brill, when you drop Jerry off. Here, I'll send this yogurt with him, just in case she's serving meat."

"Okay."

She kisses the top of my head. "Be good, honey. And give Jerry-Boy a kiss for me."

= = = = = = = = = = = = = = =

I make him eat two bowls of Cheerios, in case there isn't much for lunch. He slurps them down obediently, happy that I don't question his decision by the light of day. Then we walk to Mrs. Brill's. She's not that surprised by Jerry's news. "Peanut butter—that's the answer!" she says cheerfully. "And I have plenty of it!"

= = = = = = = = = = = = = = =

I tell Shannon at the Laundromat. She sits across from me at the orange Formica table, shaking her head. "I agree with your mom—your dad should have known better. Now you'll have to cook two meals every night."

"Can't he just have grilled cheese?"

"Two much saturated fat." Shan and her mother have to watch their weight.

"But Jerry's skinny—"

"His veins can clog up all the same." She sets aside a pile of towels. "We've got to deliver that underwear, you know."

= = = = = = = = = = = = = = =

I tell Shan about Jim. We're at McDonald's. Before I'm halfway through, she raises her eyebrows.

"Why's he talking to Jerry?"

"I don't know. Maybe he thought Jerry saw something."

"Maybe . . ." She gets lines over her eyebrows when she's thinking hard. "But it seems wrong, worrying a seven-year-old. I mean, Jerry doesn't even know what happened, right?"

"Right."

"So Jim could be the one to tell him. That would be awful."

"He won't. I told him Jerry didn't know."

"That's good." She's hesitant. "I think maybe Jerry's going to turn out like Uncle Mac—a little bit strange. . . ."

"We're going to the Exxon this afternoon. Want to come?"

She looks at me like I'm nuts, too. "Gasoline and cat pee aren't my favorite smells, especially mixed."

We dip the last couple of fries in ketchup. It's always a little sad when the carton's empty. "Daddy and Junie had an argument," Shan says.

"What about?"

"Junie's changed so much. Last summer he read out loud to us and planted a garden. This year all he does is lie around looking hateful. Then at night he leaves and goes wherever he pleases."

"Like where?"

"Wherever his so-called friends go." She looks away. "Somebody told Dad they saw him at KFC with Kyle and Jay."

Shan goes on: "That doesn't mean he's tight with them, you know? He and Kyle go way back. They played rec basketball for years. . . ." I watch her hands creasing the french fry box, folding it carefully as if there's something precious inside. "I tried to talk to him after the argument. He wouldn't open his door."

"What would you have said?"

"I don't know. But mean as Junie's acting, he's still my brother. It's easy to worry about Jerry, 'cause he's little and cute. Junie's a different story. And once he gets stuck with those kids—they can pull you down."

I know what she's talking about. Lots of boys have come up through the neighborhood, boys who were nice or at least okay until they reached a certain age. Then one day they stopped talking to you, and if you spoke to them, they'd sneer and turn away. Some went off into a crowd and never came back. Now and then you got reports through the grapevine— in juvie, wounded, working for the Job Corps. Others dropped out of school and showed up in the alleys. A few joined gangs that specialized in stealing cars or running crack.

"Junie was cute," Shan says. "I remember. He had a first-grade teacher sort of like Mrs. Brill, and he was her favorite 'cause he was so cute."

= = = = = = = = = = = = = =

Uncle Mac's under a Buick with just his legs sticking out. I crouch down and yell, "Can Jerry help you feed the cats?"

"Been fed."

"Can he pat them?"

"Them that he can catch."

"Somebody's here for gas, Uncle Mac."

His leg shifts under the car. "Go find out how much he wants, then take the money and bring it here."

Jerry loves this. He comes running back with a ten and two ones. "Twelve of regular on number three."

"Can you punch it in?"

"Yep."

"Charlie, you go with him, okay?"

We punch it in, then wave for the man in the Saab to go ahead. He's white, well dressed. He gets out of the car and comes strolling over. "I need someone to watch my little girl for ten minutes. Can you do it? I'll give you five dollars. . . ."

I'm surprised, because he doesn't know me. But maybe he noticed how grown-up Jerry and I seem running the gas station and was impressed. That idea makes me feel good. "Sure." I nod. Instantly he smiles. He looks relieved.

"Her name's Sara. Sara, come here."

She's a cute kid: dark, curly hair and green eyes. She's looking at the pavement so I guess she's shy. I crouch down: "I'm Charlie, and this is my brother Jerry. Want to stay with us for a couple minutes?"

She doesn't answer.

"There's cats here. Want to know their names?"

She nods. Her father waves and gets inside his car. "Back in a few," he calls out the window. Jerry and I play with her. She's quiet at first, then she starts to relax. I carry her around and show her everything, get her some pretzels from the snack machine. She chases after the cats, giggling. In a while Uncle Mac comes out from under the Buick.

"Who's this?"

"Her dad asked me to look after her for ten minutes."

"Hummmmph." He wipes his greasy hands on his coveralls. He tries not to look at the little girl. She's so cute he'd have to smile if she caught his eye. Just then, somebody else comes in for gas, and he goes to get the money and punch it in. "It's been longer than ten minutes," Jerry says.

"Not much longer." Sara's so cute I don't really mind. Her dad comes back a little later. He gives me a ten-dollar bill instead of a five. "Thanks. You saved my life," he says. "What did you say your name was?"

"Charlie."

"If you're here again, would you look after Sara? I sell products to a couple of stores up the street."

"Sure. She's real cute—and good, too."

"She sure is." Her dad tickles her. She smiles then and puts her arms around him. A minute later they're gone. Uncle Mac stares after them.

"Nice Saab," Jerry says.

I'm thinking of the little girl. She was so shy, so cute. I hope he brings her back again.

= = = = = = = = = = = = = =

Shan thinks the dad was irresponsible. It's the next day, almost noon; we're sitting at McDonald's. That's when she says the father shouldn't have done it, which makes me kind of mad.

"You think I wouldn't take good care of her?" Shan babysits more than me because people think she's more mature.

"You'd probably take good care of her—sounds like you did—but he didn't know that."

"He saw Jerry and me running the gas station. That made him think I was responsible."

Shan shrugs. She picks up the plastic bag with Mr. Molloy's underwear inside.

= = = = = = = = = = = = = =

He lives on Winston Avenue. The street has stucco houses with wood and glass front porches. There're some white people living here; they're older and have flower and vegetable gardens with picket fences. One lady watches Shan and me like we've got signs saying "thieves" around our necks. We go from house to house, studying the numbers. "Who are you looking for?" she asks. Her voice is high and reedy.

"Mr. Molloy."

"The large gentleman who walks with a cane?"

We nod.

"He's out right now."

"We don't need to see him," Shan tries to explain. "We have something to drop off."

"What?"

"Uhhh. . . ." She looks at me.

"A package," I mutter. "Which house is his?"

"I'm not at liberty to tell you that."

"We'll find it on our own." I stick my tongue out. The old lady retreats inside. Through the porch window we see her picking up the phone.

"Charlie, she's calling the police."

"Because I stuck out my tongue?" I'm not afraid. I keep reading the house numbers. "It's this one, right here."

= = = = = = = = = = = = = = =

Funny—as often as we've laughed at Mr. Molloy for being fat, his house is nicer than either Shan's or mine. Through the porch windows you can see shelves filled with books and a pitcher with real sunflowers inside. A case of tiny glass animals sparkles in the sun. The yard is neat, with a birdbath sitting in the middle of a patch of ivy and a little cement dragon next to that. A brass nameplate's screwed into the door: EDWARD MOLLOY III AND TUYEN CHAO. We try to shove the plastic bag through the mail slot, but it won't fit. Finally Shan tucks it behind a potted plant on the wide steps. "I'll call and let him know I left it there," she says.

"Shan, look"—I'm pointing at the closed-in porch. High in one corner, in a silver cage, are three small birds, and one of them is yellow, just like Jess.

Eleven

I drag Shan inside Dollar Discount to visit Jess. They moved her to a different cage, all by herself, and I think that she looks lonely. Her yellow seems a little faded, almost greenish. I whistle, trying to get her to sing. She looks back at me, eyes sharp, but she doesn't make a sound.

= = = = = = = = = = = = = =

This afternoon I go into the alley and look for Jim. He's not there, so I sit down and wait. Twenty minutes later I see him near the end of the block. I call and wave. He startles like one of Uncle Mac's stray cats. Then he sees it's me.

"I came yesterday," he scolds. "Where were you?"

"I didn't know I was supposed to meet you."

"I thought you were serious about this."

"I am."

His eyes bore into mine. "You have to come. We can't do anything unless you come."

"What are we going to do?"

"Investigate the suspects."

"But who *are* they?" I'm feeling shivers on my arms and legs.

"They're the ones who came into his house, the ones he knew. Because whoever it was, he opened the door to them."

I don't understand. He shakes his hands for emphasis.

"At night the door was always locked."

"Maybe they broke in."

"There was no sign of forced entry."

My heart is beating fast. He's thought of things I haven't. "Who, then?"

"Everyone he knew."

"But his friends were good."

"You don't understand." His body is trembling, and his face comes close to mine.

"What?"

"They have two sides. By day they're innocent. By night they're something else."

I want to run away, but he's holding my arm. "You understand now?" he asks.

I nod, wanting him to let go.

"You're not backing out, are you?" His hand tightens its grip.

"Uh . . . unh-uh."

"You can't back out, not now. We have to find out who it was. Everything depends on it."

I nod again. He sighs, takes the little black book out of his pocket, and opens it. "Which one do you want? Ms. Essie Smith?"

I'm too freaked out to say anything. Finally I mumble, "All right."

"Report back tomorrow. Don't be late."

"What kind of information should I bring?"

"Find out her alibi. Ask if she was home and whether she saw or heard anything unusual that night. Write the response in her own words, exactly as she says them." His grip has loosened now. "I'll see you tomorrow."

= = = = = = = = = = = = = =

Ms. Essie smiles when Jerry and I stop by. She gives us coconut cake and milk, and we sit on the glider on the front porch of her duplex. She asks Jerry about his day.

"We walked to the park. I saw a Saturn wagon and three Jettas." He tells Ms. Essie about his new diet. She doesn't laugh at him. "Good for you for living according to your beliefs."

I don't know how to ask about Mr. Healy, but it's my assignment, and it does make sense. Only by eliminating the good people will we be able to question whoever's left.

"Ms. Essie?"

She looks up.

"What were you doing when Mr. Healy died?"

"Oh, Charlie . . ." Her face changes, goes soft, and I'm sorry I asked. She takes a Kleenex from a flowered box. "You miss him, too," she says.

I nod.

"I haven't gotten over it—his death, I mean." She gives me a look, as if she understands that she can't say the truth in front of Jerry. "I was sitting right here, watching *The Late Show*—I'd been over for ice cream that very night, and we'd had such a nice talk. When I left to go home, he put his cheek close to mine. 'Essie, I love that smell,' he said. 'Is that Chanel?'" Tears stream down her cheeks, but her voice stays steady. "What a loss," she says.

Jerry looks up and sees she's crying. He's been in his own world, but he sits beside her now, puts his hand on her arm. "Don't cry."

"It's okay, sugar. Sometimes crying helps what ails us."

"What ails us?" Jerry asks.

She smiles then. "Nothing to do with you. You're as nice a boy as ever I've met, and I've known a good number of them over the years. . . ."

= = = = = = = = = = = = = = = =

We go on home. "Why was she crying, Charlie?" Jerry asks me on the way.

"If you'd listened, you'd know."

"But I didn't *know* I was supposed to listen. I was playing the peg-jumping game, and I got it down to three. What *was* it?" Jerry asks again.

"She misses Mr. Healy."

"I do, too." He's dragging the toes of his sneakers, and I kick at his foot to make him stop. "I know why people have to die," he says.

"How come?"

"To make room for the babies. There's only a certain amount of food and places to live, and if everybody stayed alive forever, the new ones couldn't come."

"Who told you that?"

"Nobody. I figured it out one night before I fell asleep. That's when I like to think about things."

He starts scraping his toes again.

"Cut that out, Jerry. It ruins your sneakers, and I hate the noise it makes."

"When are we going back to Uncle Mac's? Today?" He tugs at my hand.

"Maybe tomorrow."

"Then you can ask him, too."

"Ask him what?"

"About Mr. Healy."

"Why would I— Jerry?" I turn him so I can see into his eyes. I always know when Jerry's lying. "Have you been talking to Jim?"

"Not lately." He's looking to the side.

"You stay away from him."

"How come?"

"You're not supposed to talk to strangers."

"He isn't a stranger. Anyway, you talked to him, too."

"I had a reason. He's trying to find out something that I want to know."

"What?"

"About Mr. Healy."

"What he died from?"

"Something like that."

"What if Bobo died, Charlie?"

"He didn't."

"Would you miss him, if he did?"

"Of course I would."

"But we wouldn't eat him, not like people eat cows." Jerry starts sucking his thumb.

"Cut it out. You're way too old for that."

"Sorry." He looks up suddenly, grins. "Sometimes it helps me think."

Twelve

Junie's on the street. That's unusual lately. Jerry's all excited to see him, like he hasn't even noticed Junie's changed. "Junior, Junior!" he shrieks. Junie looks around like he's not sure where all the noise is coming from. Jerry races up and stops in front of him. I can't believe how tall Junie is. The only times I see him, he's lying on the couch.

"Hey, shorty."

"Junior, I saw a Z3 yesterday! It was on York Road, and it was blue!"

"That's cool."

"You still saving for a car?"

Junie shakes his head.

"I thought you *were*. 'Member, you said I could go with you to pick it out?"

Junie nods. His voice is flat. "I didn't understand some

things back then. Cars cost a lot of money. I'm not going to have that much anytime soon."

Jerry's disappointed. "I have seven dollars and ninety-three cents. I'll give it to you, if you want. . . ."

"That's okay, shorty." The edge of Junie's mouth twitches, like it wants to smile. He makes a fist and gives Jerry a gentle tap on the arm, and Jerry gets ready to wrestle, like they used to when Jerry was little. Back then Junie'd put on a show and then let Jerry win. But he must see something over Jerry's head, because suddenly he straightens up and his eyes narrow. I look back to see what's going on. Kyle's crossing the street toward us. His hood is pulled up, even though it's summer.

"Waz up, man?"

"Nada."

They slap hands. "C'mon," Kyle says. But Jerry wants attention. He pulls on Junie's sleeve.

"Don't you want to see my Matchbox cars?"

"Not now." The older boys laugh and turn away. They walk right past me on the sidewalk. Junie doesn't speak. I can't see Kyle's face, but I know what it looks like: sleepy, with distant, angry eyes. He nods from under his hood. When he was at Saint Mary's, I used to share my dessert with him. Maybe he hasn't forgotten that. But his voice is bored.

"Hey, Charlie."

"Hey." I turn and watch as they saunter down the street toward the corner.

= = = = = = = = = = = = = =

That night Mom chooses a video. For once it isn't Disney,
even though it stars some kids. She must not have read the
box carefully, because partway through the movie they find
a dead boy lying near some railroad tracks. They don't
know what to do, in case they get in trouble, and they don't
know who killed him, either. I see Mom and Dad sneak worried glances over Jerry's head, but he's into the movie, sitting bolt upright and staring. Once Mom says, "Jerr . . ."

"No, I want to see this."

"It won't wake you up?"

"No."

Funny, but I think it might wake me. My folks have no
idea how I'm feeling: as if Jim's hand is gripping my arm.
Ms. Essie's tears burn in my mind, like it's my fault she's so
sad. I scoot closer to my mom. She rests one hand on my
knee, passes me the popcorn with the other. Suddenly I
want to tell them what's going on. But the movie's playing—the kind of movie I asked for—and they're all into it,
so I just sit there watching.

= = = = = = = = = = = = = =

Jerry does wake up, but he doesn't tell them because he's
embarrassed. So he comes into my room in the night and
stands beside the bed. I wake up, startled, and see him there.

"What the heck are you doing?"

"Shhhh." He puts his finger to his lips.

"Answer!"

"I couldn't sleep."

"No duh." I sit up, rubbing my eyes. "Don't expect me to sit in that rocking chair with you!"

"I know." He looks sad, but I don't care. "Charlie . . ."

"What?"

"Let's go for a walk."

"Now? It's the middle of the night."

He shrugs, like that's no big deal. "We could take Bobo."

"Mom and Dad would kill us if they knew."

"How would they find out?"

"They might hear us."

He's silent for a moment. "We could sit on the front porch. That wouldn't be bad, would it?"

"I guess not. Why do you want to be outside?"

"I want to feel the dark against my skin."

"Jerry, you're so weird."

But I get up, put a sweater over my pajama top, and hand him one. "I'll unlock the door. You wait on the porch while I get Bobo. And don't you dare make a sound."

He nods, happy.

= = = = = = = = = = = = = = =

It's not that dark out, because of the streetlights, but I guess it's dark enough for Jerry. Bobo's happy, too. He wags his tail and grunts, sitting between us, then he thumps himself down to watch whatever's going on. Which is nothing. From the corner by the shopping strip we hear the gentle *whoosh* of cars. Some kind of bugs are singing in the trees.

"I like them," Jerry whispers. Bobo wags his tail.

"Has your skin felt enough dark?"

"Almost."

"What bothered you in the movie?"

"The dead boy's face."

"Why didn't you look away?"

"I meant to, but I forgot."

We sit a minute longer. "It bothered me, too," I tell him then, and he smiles, a big, crooked smile.

"That's because we're brother and sister, isn't it, Charlie?"

Bobo doesn't seem to mind going into his doghouse. I hurry back, slip the door open, and we slide silently inside.

Thirteen

The Laundromat's so hot, you stick to everything you touch. I shift in the orange plastic chair and pull my shorts lower to cover the backs of my thighs. Shan's sweating, too. I tell her about Jerry and me on the front porch. She purses her lips: "That's not safe, Charlie." I hate it when she acts like I'm a little kid. But before I can argue, Mr. Tibby comes in with a stack of newspapers.

"Good morning, Charles." Mr. Louras buys a paper, puts it on the counter for the people using self-service.

Mr. Tibby buttons the dollar into his shirt pocket. "Glad to be of service. Have a good day, one and all." He backs out.

"It's safe on my front porch." I return to the argument, but my heart isn't in it. I have to tell Shannon about Jim.

Maybe she senses there's something else, because once

we get to McDonald's, she looks me in the eyes and says, "What's up?"

"I talked to Jim again. Now he wants to question everybody that knew Mr. Healy, and find out their alibis." I'm ashamed to tell about Ms. Essie, but I do. "I knew she didn't have anything to do with it. She started crying."

"People say they liked each other."

"I'm going back today to tell him what she said."

"So you can say she had nothing to do with it."

I feel lame. "He . . . he held my arm."

"What do you mean?"

"Just for a moment, he wouldn't let me go."

She shakes her head. "You ought to stay away from him."

"Going through the suspects one by one isn't a bad idea. It gives us a chance to eliminate them. Then we can focus on whoever's left."

"Next you'll be questioning me."

I laugh. "He hasn't mentioned you so far."

"I think you ought to stay away from him."

"Maybe." But I know I won't.

= = = = = = = = = = = = = =

I meet him that afternoon. He seems more relaxed, and he smiles when I give him the piece of paper that tells what

Ms. Essie said. "She's really nice," he admits. "But for protocol, we have to interview everyone."

"That's what I thought."

He scribbles something in his pocket notebook. "Who do you want next?" he asks.

"Who's left?"

"That old man Arthur played chess with and Mrs. Bridges—she said she was asleep, but we ought to talk to her—and those kids who hung around. . . ."

I don't wait for him to get to Shannon, because it'll be just like she said. "I'll take Uncle Mac," I say quickly.

"Why do you call him that?"

"I don't know. All us kids do."

"He's not a relative?"

"No."

"You can't interview your own relatives. You couldn't be objective." He looks at me hard.

His statement reminds me of something. I shift from foot to foot. "Remember when we talked about Jerry?"

Jim looks nervous for a second, like I've accused him of doing something wrong. "I didn't tell."

"The best thing would be if you'd just leave him alone. He's sensitive, and there's a lot he doesn't understand."

"There's a lot most of us don't. The devil works in strange ways."

"I know, but could you leave him alone, please?"

His eyes stare into mine. "Jerry's important. The plan won't work without him."

"What do you mean by that?"

"Nothing. Just do what I say and don't tell anyone."

"Not even Shannon?"

"No one. I'll see you here tomorrow, at this same time." He snaps the notebook shut. "Don't be late."

= = = = = = = = = = = = = =

I go around the corner and sit down on the steps of an apartment house. My stomach's lurching. *The plan won't work without him.* . . . Jim talked like he knew something about Jerry that I don't. What could he possibly know about my little brother?

= = = = = = = = = = = = = =

When I pick Jerry up this afternoon, I hold his hand. He tries to shake me off. "Charlie, that's too tight."

I don't answer.

"Didn't you hear me? You're squishing me."

"Hush, Jerry."

"Can't we go to Uncle Mac's?"

"Not today."

"You said!"

I remember then that I'm supposed to question him. "All right."

"Good!" He tries to run ahead, but I won't let him go.

= = = = = = = = = = = = = =

Uncle Mac's brushing cats from under the hood of an old Sentra, then poking around inside. "Could be the belts," he says to no one in particular. "But maybe not."

Jerry pulls on the old man's coverall. "Can I feed the cats?"

"I guess. Wait till I finish here, then I'll tell you who gets what."

We sit on a workbench. The dank, cool garage feels good after the hot air outside. In a minute, Uncle Mac backs out from under the hood and looks up blinking, like a turtle who's been inside his shell. "How you kids doing?" he asks.

"Good," Jerry says. I don't answer.

"That man was looking for you, Charlie," he says then.

My heart goes thump. "What man?"

"The one with the little girl. He wanted you to watch her yesterday."

"Oh, Sara's dad."

"Went down the street and left her in the car all by herself while I was changing the oil. I nearly called the cops on him."

"How come?"

"Just 'cause I've got cats I'm in the kid business, too?"

"It was probably only for a minute."

"More like ten. I've got a notion what the fellow's up to."

"What?"

"Never you mind." He slams a pair of pliers down on the counter and swears out loud. Jerry's eyes get big. We hardly ever hear Uncle Mac cuss. But he goes and opens the refrigerator, same as usual, and pulls out milk and day-old bread. "Get the pans, Jerry."

Jerry does. They load them up, sprinkle cat chow on top. Jerry opens one car at a time and shoves the dish of food onto the floor mat. In the meantime cats pour in to eat from the aluminum pans Uncle Mac puts on the office floor. He greets them gruffly: "Hey, Brownie, Cisco, Angel." A few curl around his legs and purr, and he bends and rubs the spot between their ears. "Eat, now. I ain't got all day."

"Uncle Mac?"

"What?" He's picking up a socket wrench, adjusting the head.

"When Mr. Healy died, what were you doing?"

He grunts, startled, maybe, that I'm asking. "I don't know—I was asleep or opening up the shop, I guess. I heard the ambulance, but that ain't nothing around here. Then Essie called. She was all broke up, you know."

He doesn't look me in the face. Uncle Mac is shy about feelings.

"Do you think they'll catch who did it?"

"How should I know?" He shrugs, like the question's not important. "I can't do nothing."

"But you cared about him."

"Don't go there. . . ." He shakes his head, even though he's looking the other way. "Leave that alone, Charlie."

= = = = = = = = = = = = = = =

On the way home Jerry and I go to Dollar Discount. Jess isn't singing, and some of her feathers look raggedy. She's still in a cage by herself. I ask the salesclerk why. She shrugs. "Maybe it's sick."

"She's probably lonely. You should put her back with the parakeets. She liked that better."

"Who are you—my boss?"

"No, but I know what she likes."

"You kids ain't supposed to hang around here without any money. I see you in front of that birdcage every other day, and you never buy a thing."

"I buy gum. And I'm going to buy my brother a Tootsie Pop right now."

"You are?" Jerry's face lights up. "I didn't know that."

"Take your time, and pick the one you want."

He hustles over and grabs a sour apple. I plunk the quarter on the counter. The clerk smirks as she rings up the sale.

"Thanks, Charlie." Jerry's thrilled. He has no idea I bought the stupid thing to make a point. "Are we going home now?" he asks.

But I turn Jerry toward Winston Avenue. We poke along, him staring at everything in sight and me hoping the woman who got mad at Shan and me before is in her house. She is. I walk past Mr. Molloy's. The light's on in the sunporch, and a late-model Chevy's parked in front of the house. "Nice car." Jerry checks it out. "Malibu 350, 2002."

"Come with me."

"How come?"

"I'm going to ring the bell." Out of the corner of my eye I see the birds fluttering in their cage.

"Who lives here?"

"Mr. Molloy."

"A fat man with a Chinese wife?"

"Don't say fat. He might be able to hear us."

"How come you're talking to him?"

"He's got birds. Maybe he'll know what's wrong with Jess."

Jerry nods. He understands his role; he holds my hand and tries to look cute. I push the doorbell, then bang the heavy knocker. For a minute nothing happens. Then the door opens slowly. He's standing just inside, wearing pants and a silky-looking robe that's tied around his huge middle. His face is like a bulldog, with saggy jowls. He examines us. Finally he says, "Yes?"

"I'm Charlene—the one who bought you the new underwear. I just wanted to make sure you got it, and that it fit all right."

His eyes flicker.

"If it didn't, we'll exchange it for you. It's only a short bus ride. We want to know you're satisfied, 'cause the whole thing was just an unfortunate accident." I'd learned that phrase from TV.

"Where's Shannon?" His face is like a mask.

"She couldn't come. But this is my little brother, Jerry."

Jerry looks up and smiles. The Tootsie Pop stick poking out of his mouth makes him look sort of silly.

"Well, the underwear is completely satisfactory, and I thank you for replacing it." Little ripples have started across the robe, like maybe he's going to be sick. He starts to shut the door.

"Wait!"

A strangling noise comes from his throat, then he starts to bellow. It takes me a second to realize he's laughing. I stand there like a fool, not knowing what to do or say. The laughter subsides slowly, like waves turning little by little to still water. He wipes his eyes with the sleeve of his robe. "I beg your pardon," he says. "Is there something else?"

I nod. "There's this bird—she's in a cage at Dollar Discount, and I visit her every couple of days, and now I think she might be sick. And when we brought the underwear I noticed you have birds. . . ."

After all the stuff with Jim, I start sniffling over *this*. A couple of tears roll down my face, and I wipe them away quick, hoping he won't see. Jerry gets upset. "Charlie," he murmurs, "poor Charlie."

The big man's eyes are kind. "What sort of bird is she?"

"She's a canary, and they put her in a cage all by herself. She doesn't like that, so she won't sing. Her feathers are messed up, and she's changing color, too."

"Molting. Where is she, again?"

"Dollar Discount."

He shakes his head. "They shouldn't be allowed to keep animals."

"Could you check on her?"

"I can't promise, but I'll try."

"Thank you!"

I grab Jerry's arm—he's still staring up at Mr. Molloy— and we hurry away.

Fourteen

That night I watch Jerry like a hawk. Twice I get up to make sure he's still in bed where he's supposed to be. In the morning, when I wake him, he's the same as ever, sleepy and slow. He thinks I'm nervous about Jess. "Maybe he'll visit her," he says. "The cage with the other birds was nice. I like the way he had them on the sunporch, so they could see the trees."

"Hurry up, Jerry. We have to leave in ten minutes."

"I'm almost done." He slurps down the last of his Cheerios and starts putting on his sneakers. He does things in slow motion. Then he has to find his glasses. I stand there tapping my foot. Finally he's ready, and I drag him off to Mrs. Brill's.

= = = = = = = = = = = = = =

Shannon knows something's wrong. "You talked to him again, didn't you?" she asks.

"Unh-uh." Blood rushes to my face.

"Yes, you did. But you won't admit it, 'cause I told you not to do it and you know I'm right."

"What are you, my mother?" She's getting on my nerves.

"No, Charlie. I'm your friend."

"If you're my friend, you'll shut up about the whole thing." I don't realize how loud my voice is. Some of the people in the other booths at McDonald's turn and stare. Shan is furious.

"Since when do you tell me to shut up?"

"Since you started getting into my business when I asked you not to." My heart is pounding in my throat.

"You didn't ask me not to!"

"I am now!"

She knows something's wrong. "Charlie, what happened?"

"Leave me alone!" With my own words echoing in my ears, I get up and walk away.

= = = = = = = = = = = = = =

Shan and I have fought like sisters over books, movies, clothes, and games. The worst fight happened years ago, when we were playing Barbies on Mr. Healy's porch. All that morning I'd had Barbie, and Shan was stuck with Ken. When it was time to switch, I decided to go home instead. We started screaming at each other, and the next thing I knew, I'd grabbed Shan's Little Princess Barbie, pulled her head off, and thrown it in the hedge. Mr. Healy must have heard the fuss, 'cause a minute later he was standing in front of us, asking what was going on.

Shan held up her doll. She was sobbing so hard she couldn't speak. She pointed to me, then to the hedge.

"Charlie—"

"I'm going home!"

"Not quite yet." His voice was firm. "I'm too old and stiff to crawl around inside those bushes."

"But she—"

"We'll talk about that later. Right now we have to get the doll's head back before it dies."

He waited, hands on hips. Somehow I knew I'd be in trouble if I didn't cooperate. Frowning as big and mean as I could, I dug around inside that stupid hedge. "There's poison ivy in here. I'm allergic to that."

He didn't answer.

"If I get it, my parents will be really mad."

Silence. Then I saw the head and grabbed it. The hair was all messed up, which made me happy. I dropped it into his hands and went right home, like I'm doing now.

= = = = = = = = = = = = = =

Jim is there exactly on time. He's got his little notebook open. "What did you find out?" he asks.

I tell him what Uncle Mac said.

"He could be lying. The devil has many voices. His tongue can be sweet as honey when he needs it to."

"But Uncle Mac and Mr. Healy were close friends. They played chess with each other almost every night."

"That could have been a ploy. Maybe all that time he was planning to come in and steal something."

"Why would he? All he cares about is cats."

"Maybe he needed money."

"He doesn't. He owns the Exxon free and clear. And he's got those old cars, too."

"They're ruined—everyone knows that. He let the cats inside, and they soiled the upholstery." Jim leans over. His face seems to grow larger right in front of me, until it's all that I can see. "You don't understand," he says.

"What?"

"They're tricking us until they find out what we know. Then they'll try to kill us, too."

"Not me—I'm just a kid!" My mind is turning flips.

"You sound like the rest of them—not taking responsibility, always making excuses for what happens." He flips the notebook shut and sticks it back inside his pocket. "Tomorrow," he says.

"No, I don't want to."

"What about your brother?"

"What about him?"

"You should do this for him."

"You leave Jerry alone."

"I'm not going to hurt him. I just want to make sure that other people don't."

"Nobody's going to hurt my brother!"

"Everybody will get hurt if we don't hurry. On the last day, the Day of Judgment, this world will end in flames." His voice is softer, like he knows that I'm afraid.

"You're crazy." I didn't mean to say the words out loud, and I'm not sure that he hears them.

He just smiles and walks away.

= = = = = = = = = = = = = =

When I go to Mrs. Brill's this afternoon. Jerry's playing on the swing set with the other kids. He doesn't have the faintest idea what's happening. "Hi, Charlie," he says, waving at me. "Look how high I am!"

"Don't do that, Jerry. It's dangerous!"

"No, it isn't. I do it all the time."

"You could fall and break your neck."

He keeps on swinging. Mrs. Brill nods at me from her lawn chair. She's got two kids in her lap, and she's reading a story to them. She looks up and smiles. "He had a good day."

My voice is shaking, but I can't tell her why I'm so upset. "Could you please make sure Jerry doesn't talk to any strangers? Could you keep an extra-special eye on him, for the next few days?"

She looks concerned. "Is there something I should know about?"

"Oh, no." I swallow. "It's just that . . . he's so innocent, you know? Someone could take advantage of him."

"I won't let that happen." She puts her hand on mine. The warmth is like a fireplace on a cold, cold night. She notices. "Goodness, you're clammy, Charlie. Are you sure you feel okay?"

I force a smile. "I'm fine."

= = = = = = = = = = = = = =

Jerry wants to go to Uncle Mac's, but I head him straight toward home. Marcus rides by doing wheelies, his great big pumpkin-head smile flashing as he passes. "Hey, Jerr, want to ride with me?"

"Yeah."

I interrupt. "He can't. We have stuff to do at home."

"I don't either." Jerry wiggles free. He's thrilled that Marcus asked him, because Marcus is older.

Marcus doesn't believe me anyway. "Like what?"

"Like none of your business."

"You kids— Is that dog chained up?" It's Mr. Vargas, in his mail truck. He opens the door and leans out. "Have you seen Jim Chalmers, who used to live with Arthur Healy?

Somebody told me he was back. He didn't leave a forwarding address, and I have a stack of mail for him at the post office."

"I can take it. I see him all the time."

"Why don't you just tell him? Or if he can't come because of work, he can write a note giving you permission to pick it up."

"All right. I'll tell him that."

But as I walk away, a plan takes root inside my mind.

≡ ≡ ≡ ≡ ≡ ≡ ≡ ≡ ≡ ≡ ≡ ≡ ≡ ≡

Maybe Jim is right, about good and evil. 'Cause I used to be a good kid—not perfect, but at least okay. Tonight I'm thinking about stuff that's definitely wrong. Not just thinking. I may do it, too.

≡ ≡ ≡ ≡ ≡ ≡ ≡ ≡ ≡ ≡ ≡ ≡ ≡ ≡

"Bless me, Father . . . I have committed the sin of theft."

"What did you steal?"

"Somebody else's mail. But there was a reason."

"What was that?"

"He threatened my little brother."

"Why would he do that?"

"Because he's mad at me, because I said I'd help him figure out who killed this other man. . . ."

"What man was that?"

"He lived on my block."

"How old are you, my child?"

"I just turned thirteen."

"Don't you know the difference between truth and stories?"

= = = = = = = = = = = = = =

I sit on my bed a while longer, looking out the window. Then I write this note:

> *To whom it may concern:*
> *Please give my mail to Charlene Poggio. I can't*
> *pick it up cause I'm at work.*
>
> *Jim Chalmers*

Fifteen

I'm calmer the next morning, more determined. After I drop Jerry off, I go straight to the post office. I tell the clerk what Mr. Vargas said. Maybe because I mention his name, the note works like a charm. She comes back to the counter with a pile of envelopes and gives them all to me.

= = = = = = = = = = = = = =

His mail is mostly junk, form letters begging for money, pizza ads, the same flyers we throw out each week. There are a few that look like bills. The personal ones are from Port Arthur, Texas, with the same return address: Marie Chalmers, 641 Reyes Street. The handwriting of the sender is large and sloping, like an older person's. I slide a knife under the back lip of an envelope and open it.

Dearest son,

I have been worried after not hearing from you for so long. I called the hospital, but they would tell nothing of your whereabouts, so that now I do not even know if you are still on Lanvale Street. Please call me collect, or write telling me where you are.

How are you doing, Jim? Are you remembering to take your medicine? Are you able to work? Do you need money?

I sent you underwear and socks when you wrote you needed them. Did they get to you all right?

All here is as usual. Tom has a job in a restaurant on Tolman Street, cooking breakfast and lunch. The weather has been hot. We bought a new air conditioner and put it in the upstairs hall window.

Love,
Mother

I read the letter twice, feeling ashamed. It sounds like Jim's been sick. Did Mr. Healy mention there was something wrong with him? Could he have cancer or another disease? Does he wear the raincoat to cover something up?

I feel too guilty to open the other letters. Maybe I'll give him those and act like I picked them up to do him a favor.

For now, I leave them in my room. I want to make up with Shan. She should be leaving the Laundromat, headed for McDonald's, just about now.

I walk past Mrs. Brill's on my way there. What I see makes me freeze.

Jim's in the yard with the children. Mrs. Brill is there, too, talking with him while he pushes Maya in the swing. He's pushing her high, but Mrs. Brill sees it and slows it with one hand. Jerry's on top of the jungle gym. I squat behind the hedge, peer through.

"It was a terrible thing, the worst that's happened around here, and I've lived in this neighborhood since I was ten."

Jim nods. Mrs. Brill goes on.

"You've been around here for a while, but I never knew what kind of work you did."

"I work part-time for HDL."

"I haven't heard of them."

"The work is off and on—filing and sorting. Before then I worked construction in Port Arthur, Texas. That's my home."

He pushes the swing again, too hard. "I had to get away. There were problems at my job—"

"I'm hot," Jerry interrupts. His voice is squeaky.

"Mrs. B., I have to go to the bathroom!" someone calls.

"I'll be right there."

"I'll stay here with them," Jim says quickly. I almost jump out of my skin. But she shakes her head.

"It's snack time, anyway. Children, come inside so you can wash up and have your juice and crackers."

"Juice and crackers!" They're happy. Jerry's voice blends right in. From the bathroom that same kid is squealing, "I need help!"

"Nice to see you again, Jim," Mrs. Brill says. "I hope what I told you is helpful."

He jots down something in his notebook, starts to leave. I quickly scoot over behind the old garage. But Jim goes out the gate and hurries down the alley without looking back.

= = = = = = = = = = = = = =

Shannon doesn't smile when she sees me come in, and just before I sit down, a boy beats me to it. He slides over in the booth, grins right at Shan. "Charlie, this is Ray," she says. She seems embarrassed, but he acts like he's known her all his life.

"Hey," he greets me. "How you doing?"

"Okay." I don't know what to do.

"He goes to Western, and he wants to be premed, like me."

"That's cool."

"Charlie goes to Saint Mary's."

He nods. "They only go through middle school, right?"

"Yeah, I'll probably go to Western next year."

"You'll like it. It's a good school." He's nice, but my face is burning. I feel like a baby. Shan doesn't say sit down.

"I'll see you later," I murmur.

"So long, Charlie."

I stumble out the door.

= = = = = = = = = = = = = =

In the alley, Jim sees me before I can duck away. "You came—good." He opens the notebook. "I was worried you were going to quit."

I don't say anything.

"I forgot to give you an interview. Could you take that boy with the big round head?"

"Marcus?" I keep my voice level, and my eyes stay down. "Sure, okay."

"You know what to ask?"

"Where he was that night, what he was doing?"

Jim nods. "In his own words. And don't forget to ask whether he heard or saw anything unusual."

"All right."

"I'll see you tomorrow, then."

"Okay."

I walk away, but for some reason, I look back over my shoulder. Jim's watching me, arms limp against his sides, as if he's powerless. His eyes meet mine. "It all depends on this," he says.

Only later do I realize that I should have given him the letters.

= = = = = = = = = = = = = =

As soon as I get Jerry, I start in on him: "What did I tell you about Jim? And what in the world was he doing in that yard?"

His shoulders slump, like he knows he's going to get scolded. "I didn't invite him—he came inside the gate to talk to Mrs. B."

We walk on. "How did you know, anyway?" he asks.

"I—I was going past."

"I didn't see you."

"That's 'cause I hid."

"You hid? Are you afraid of Jim?"

"Maybe a little." I don't want to freak him out. "I saw him today, and he behaved okay."

"But another time he didn't?"

"He's just weird, Jerry."

"I don't think so."

"That's 'cause you have no idea what's normal."

He doesn't answer.

"Stay away from him, okay?"

We go to Uncle Mac's garage. He's just finished putting an alternator in a Toyota Camry. The owner is a woman, young, blond, and wearing a business suit. When she hears the price, she acts as if she's going to faint. "Eighty percent of it's the part," Uncle Mac explains. "I hate to fix Toyotas, 'cause the parts are all so high." He shows her the receipt from the supplier on Twenty-first Street. After that she's pleasant. She gives him a credit card, nods at Jerry and me on her way out.

More cars come in for gas. Uncle Mac lets us operate the pump and make change for the cash payments. Then the white man with the Saab comes in. He smiles when he sees me, but he's acting nervous. "Missed you the other day," he says.

"I was at home."

"Can't make much money when you're home." Before Uncle Mac can say anything, he thrusts Sara into my arms. "Be right back," he says. He doesn't kiss her good-bye.

She doesn't seem to mind. She remembers me from before, and right away she says, "Where's kitty?" Jerry finds some of the tamer cats and holds them up for her to pat. She laughs and strokes them. "Be gentle," we tell her. "Kitty, kitty . . ." She wants more. But suddenly her dad is here.

He's different from before; his hands are shaking, and his eyes look mad. He doesn't say how come he's back so soon, just hands me two dollars and grabs Sara out of my arms. He squeals out of the lot without saying good-bye. Uncle Mac looks after him. "Good riddance."

= = = = = = = = = = = = = =

Walking home, we see Marcus on his bike. He's wearing his baseball outfit from the rec league. "I'm on the Red Sox!" he brags. "We rule!"

"Marcus, come inside. I need to talk to you."

"You got anything to eat?"

"I'll look if you come in."

Sixteen

Marcus is a snoop. While I'm getting cookies from the cupboard, he pokes through our videos, then goes into Jerry's room and gets his Nerf gun and some comics. He can't read as well as Jerry, but he pretends he can. "This one ain't funny." He drops it on the floor. "Let Bobo in, Charlie." All the kids know we break the rules.

"Okay, just for a minute."

I go out to the doghouse and bring him in.

Bobo's happy to see us. He licks Jerry and me and starts running around the house. His big feet go *whomp whomp whomp* around the rooms. Marcus comes downstairs, more of Jerry's comics in one hand. In the other he's holding an envelope. It takes me a minute to realize what it is.

"What were you doing in my room?"

"Looking for another Batman comic." He shows me the one he finished. His eyes meet mine. He holds the envelope over Jerry's head, so he can't see, and mouths, "What?"

"I'm picking up his mail since he moved out."

"And reading it?"

"Uhhh . . ."

Marcus looks me in the eye. He must think that he's the king of trouble on our block. "Whaz up?"

Words stick in my throat. I'm mad at Marcus for snooping in my room, but I've known him forever, and I don't have Shan to talk to now.

"Let me put Jerry on Nintendo. Then I'll tell you."

= = = = = = = = = = = = = =

That's a treat, so Jerry doesn't object. I make him a glass of chocolate milk, put him in my room, and close the door. Then I sit Marcus on the couch.

"First, you got to swear not to open your mouth. If you do, somebody could get hurt."

He swears.

I don't know where to start. I begin with telling how Jerry and I met Jim in the alley on the way to day care. Then I tell the rest. When I get to the part about interviewing Ms. Essie and Uncle Mac, Marcus frowns.

"That's stupid. They wouldn't hurt nobody."

"He's interviewing other people, too. He plans to narrow the field, one by one, which makes sense, I think. But after a couple of days—"

"What?"

"He started saying strange stuff. And now I'm supposed to talk to you."

"Me! What about?"

"Where you were that night."

Marcus's eyes get big. "I don't know nothing."

"Don't get upset—remember, we're asking everyone." But I know how he feels. "I'm scared, 'cause of the way Jim talks," I confess.

"How'd you get his mail?"

"Mr. Vargas was looking for him, remember? He said if Jim wrote a note, they'd let me pick up his mail."

"He wrote a note?"

"No. I forged it. I thought if I could read his mail, I'd know more about him, and I could figure out a way to quit the investigation."

"Why don't you just tell him no?"

"I did. Then he threatened Jerry."

"How?"

"That's the strange part. He didn't exactly say how."

"So you opened his mail?"

"Just one." I swallow. "It's from his mom. You can read it, if you want."

"Oh, no." Marcus shakes his head so fast he reminds me of a wet dog. "Then I'll be guilty, too."

"I could read it out loud. That way it wouldn't be your fault."

= = = = = = = = = = = = = = =

Afterward he's serious. "There's something wrong. You can tell his mom is worried." He flips through the rest of the envelopes, like I did. "These are from her, too. The others look like bills."

"Should we open more?"

He pulls his knees up, rests his forehead against them. I guess that's what he does instead of sucking his thumb. "No. You know what we should do?"

"What?"

"Ask Junie."

"About what?"

"This whole thing—the letter and the investigation. He's real smart, and he's hot about what happened to Mr. Healy, too."

"He's so mean now. Half the time he doesn't even bother to say hi."

"He's just trying to act big so nobody messes with him."

"Who would pick on Junie?"

Marcus doesn't answer. He doesn't like to talk about Kyle, but a couple of times Marcus has come to school with a split lip. When I ask what happened, he'll say he fell or that a tree branch snapped back and hit him in the mouth. But now he seems to read my mind.

"Not Kyle—the punks . . ."

"The ones around the corner?"

"Them and their friends. They messed Kyle up bad."

"How come?"

"He don't tell me anything. But he could hardly walk. Jay-Jay had to bring him home and put him on the bed. Kyle said if I said one word to Aunt Lily, he'd tear me up."

"When was that?"

"Back in the spring."

"I still see him hanging out down there."

Marcus shrugs. "I guess he figured, if you can't beat 'em, join 'em."

We're quiet for a minute. I really want to talk to Shan, but I'm embarrassed to call her after our fight. So I ask Marcus to, instead.

"Why don't you call her?"

"Mind your own business."

"You two been squabbling?"

"Never." I hand him the phone.

= = = = = = = = = = = = = =

She comes over right away, and right away I tell her, "You were right."

"About what?"

"Staying away from Jim."

And then I tell her everything.

= = = = = = = = = = = = = = =

Even Shan isn't sure what to do. She finds a piece of paper, writes things down.

"He said, 'By day they're innocent, by night they're something else'?"

"I think that's how it went."

"Doesn't that remind you of something?"

"What?"

"A video we watched. *Dr. Jekyll*—"

"And Mr. Hyde." Marcus must have seen it, too. "It's like everybody's two people—one evil and one good."

Shannon nods. "But that was just a story. This is real life. And if he truly believes that—"

"What?"

She shakes her head. She's still mulling it over. After a minute she says, "Charlie, I think Jim is sick."

"We *know* he's sick. Why else would his mother ask about his pills?"

"I don't mean a regular sickness, like cancer or hepatitis," Shan says. "I think he's mentally ill."

"Mentally ill?" Marcus sounds the words out slowly, as if he's never heard of that.

"Yes. Your mind can get sick, just like your body. Some doctors think it's caused by messed-up chemicals inside your brain. To get them back to normal, you take medicine."

"Pills can't stop you being crazy." Marcus stares at her. "If they could, somebody'd put them in the water around here."

"You're right about that." We all laugh. But Shan turns serious again.

"What if I'm right, and Jim forgot to take his pills or they ran out?"

"How could we find that out? I can't exactly ask him if he's nuts."

"You could ask him if he needs to see a doctor to get more medicine . . . ," she thinks out loud. "Or we could tell some grown-up what we think."

"They'll say steer clear of him."

"I mentioned him to Junie, who said the same thing: 'Stay away from him.' "

"I can't, because of Jerry."

"Why don't we call the cops?" Marcus asks.

"Legally Jim hasn't done anything wrong."

"We could say he threatened."

"Nobody takes a kid's word over an adult's." Shan looks at Marcus. "You know that."

= = = = = = = = = = = = = = =

"We won't say nothing," Marcus says, before he leaves. Shan just looks at me.

"Coming tomorrow?"

I look down. "Yeah."

She gets ready to go, too.

"Who was that boy?" I ask.

"I introduced you." Shan's face is torn between lighting up and the worry I've given her. "He might come tomorrow. If he does, then you can talk to him."

Seventeen

In the morning I take Jerry, same as usual. Then I head back, through the alley. I'll cut across the main strip, hit Dollar Discount, and the Laundromat.

"Hey, Charlie." It's Mr. Vargas. "Where's that dog?"

"He's on his chain."

"Good. I saw that man—Jim Chalmers—and I told him you were looking for him, and I thought you had his mail."

Maybe my face changes, 'cause he looks hard at me.

"Don't worry. He said he'd find you. He seemed pleased to know you'd picked it up."

"He was?"

"Yeah. Guess he's a busy man. I gave him a change-of-address card to fill out, and he said he would."

Later I realized I should have asked Mr. Vargas when he'd seen Jim and where.

= = = = = = = = = = = = = = =

By the time I get to the Laundromat, Shan's done. She tells me right away her friend can't come. I guess he called last night and let her know.

We get our Coke and fries and find a booth. I tell Shan what Mr. Vargas said. Her eyes get serious. "What will you do?"

"I can take the mail when I meet him this afternoon—all but the letter we opened. I'll act like I'm doing him a favor. Then I'll say I can't help with the investigation anymore."

= = = = = = = = = = = = = = =

But Jim's not in the alley when I go to pick up Jerry. I shove the bag with his letters in it into my shorts so I don't have to answer questions. When I get home, I stick the bag behind the couch.

Jerry and I decide to work a puzzle on the front porch table. We pick a woodland scene with animals and wildflowers. Jerry dumps the pieces out while I get milk and candy from the kitchen. When I come back, I'm face-to-face with Jim. The tray I'm holding clatters to the floor.

He stares at me, wide-eyed. "I have the mail," I stammer. "I'll get it for you now."

"Not that— I mean, that's not why I came." He grabs me by the wrist. "They know," he whispers.

"Know what?"

"About the investigation." He keeps his voice low. Maybe he thinks that Jerry can't hear us. "They got me on the sidewalk and told me that I had to stop."

"Who?"

"The evil ones. They tried to tear my raincoat." He shows me a place where the lining's pulled away. "They didn't know it buttons on, so I can fix it back."

"Who are they?"

"I don't know their names."

I'm trembling, but when I look into his face, I see he's terrified himself. I remember suddenly what Shan said: *"I think he's mentally ill."* I struggle to control my words:

"J-J-Jim, do you maybe need to see a doctor?"

"They didn't hurt me, just the raincoat."

"Did your medicine run out?"

"Oh, my Lord." He drops my wrist abruptly, stares into my face. "They told you, didn't they?"

"No, nobody told me anything."

"Then how did you know?"

"I, uh, it was just a guess."

"They told you." A shudder passes through him, and he sags. "You're on their side now."

"I'm not on anyone's side—"

"I have to go." He backs away from me.

I stammer, "L-let me get your mail." I run inside, grab it, and run back out. He's on the sidewalk now. "Here. . . ."

He acts like it's on fire, fumbling with the envelopes, shoving them into his coat pocket. He's falling apart in front of me.

"I didn't tell them anything," I say again.

"Now it's just the two of us. Jerry and I are the only ones left."

= = = = = = = = = = = = = =

Once he leaves, I start crying. Then Jerry starts, too, and we hold each other, bawling our eyes out. We're still that way when Mom comes home. She takes one look at us and hugs us tight.

"What happened? Are you all right?"

We nod.

"What happened?" she asks again. I'm not sure where to start.

"We got scared."

"Who scared you?"

"Jim Chalmers—the raincoat man."

"What did he do? Did he hurt you?"

"No. . . ."

She waits. I tell her about the scene on the front porch, not mentioning Jim's mail. She's confused. "Why would he come here?" she asks.

"He needed help with the investigation, so I volunteered to interview Ms. Essie and Uncle Mac."

"Interview them about what?"

"Where they were the night Mr. Healy was killed, whether they heard anything—stuff like that."

"You thought that you and he could figure out what happened?"

I feel stupid now.

"You're only a child!" Mom stares at me. My heart sinks. Her words seem like a put-down or a curse.

She sighs then. "Let's wait till Dad gets home," she says. "That's only an hour. We'll talk and figure out what to do."

＝ ＝ ＝ ＝ ＝ ＝ ＝ ＝ ＝ ＝ ＝ ＝ ＝ ＝

My dad's upset. But as soon as he finds out that we're okay, the questions start.

"Why were you talking to this man?"

"Because I thought he knew things about what happened to Mr. Healy. Jim was in the house the night he died."

"And?"

"The police never caught anybody."

"And you thought you could do better?" Dad shakes his head. He leans back against the couch, looking glum. "As you get older, you'll start to accept the world's injustices and take life as it comes."

"I won't, either!"

"You think you can change things?"

"Yes!"

He sighs, then reaches over and tousles my hair. "I'm glad you weren't hurt," he whispers. He goes upstairs to take a shower.

= = = = = = = = = = = = = =

When he comes back down, his mood has changed. He wants to go find Jim "right this minute" and to take me with him. "Where does he live?" he asks.

"I don't know. We see him in the alleys."

"Which one?"

"Mostly over behind Abel, near Mrs. Brill's."

He finishes his beer and stands up. "Let's go," he says.

"Uhhh . . . there's something more."

I tell Dad about the letters, not mentioning the one I opened. His eyes practically bug right out of their sockets. "You collected his mail without his permission?"

"Uh-huh."

"It's against the law to take somebody else's property."

"Even their mail? Most of it was junk."

"Anything!" Dad glares at me. He looks over at Mom. "And he knew you had it?"

"Yes, because Mr. Vargas told him."

Dad paces back and forth, thinking. But he doesn't change his mind. "We're going to talk to Jim right now. If he's been harassing you, then seeing us together will let him know we're serious when we tell him to stop."

I want to tell Dad that there's even more: the stuff about Jerry, and the Day of Judgment, the desperate way Jim's eyes look when they're staring into mine. *"It's everywhere,"* he'd told me once. *"Only you can't see it."*

"Bring Bobo's leash," Dad says impatiently. "I want to take him, too."

= = = = = = = = = = = = = =

Sure enough, Jim's down the alley in his raincoat. His back is to us, but Dad calls his name. He startles, looks up. When he sees Dad, he freezes like an animal that sees the hunter but doesn't know which way to run.

"Mr. Chalmers." My dad sticks out his hand, and Jim shakes it. He hasn't looked toward me.

"I'm Dominic Poggio, and this is Charlie—you know her, I think. And this is our dog, Bobo."

Jim smiles nervously. "I love dogs," he says. He reaches into his pocket and gives Bobo a bit of food before Dad or I can stop him. Bobo wags his tail and licks Jim's hand. "I remember Bobo from Mr. Healy's. I used to live there, you know."

"I remember. But I never got a chance to talk to you. Arthur had so many people in and out."

Jim nods. "He'd open the door to anyone."

"That's true. He had a heart of gold." I can see by Dad's expression that this isn't what he was expecting. After a minute he clears his throat. "Charlie tells me that you're doing some detective work."

"Did she tell you that?" Jim doesn't look at me. "I'm figuring out who came to the house that night," he says. "I've almost got it solved. No one should walk away from a crime like that."

Dad nods. Then he steps forward. He's shorter than Jim, but his shoulders are squared. You can see the muscles under his T-shirt.

"I don't want Charlene involved in this," he says. "She's supposed to take care of her brother in the afternoons."

"You mean Jerry?" Jim smiles again.

"I don't want her involved," Dad repeats. He won't be distracted, and his voice is flat and still. "Arthur's death was very hard on her. She doesn't need to be reminded of it. Do you understand?"

Jim nods his head up and down, up and down. "She wanted to help," he protests softly.

"I know. Young people think they can solve all life's problems, but they can't. And sometimes we adults have to decide what's best for them."

"I understand—"

"Good. So you'll leave her alone from this point on? Not speak to her or send her notes or call her on the telephone?"

"I never called her," Jim says.

"No. And I apologize for her collecting your mail. That was a mistake on her part, and it shouldn't have happened."

"It's all right. She was trying to help me."

"So we understand each other?"

Jim nods.

"Come on, Charlie," Dad says then. We walk away without saying good-bye.

Eighteen

I talk to Shan the next morning. We're sitting in the Laundromat, drinking ice water from the refrigerator in the back office. I tell her about Jim coming to the house, what we told our folks, and Dad's conversation with him in the alley. "You were right—he's crazy."

Shan nods when the story's over, but she sounds unsure. "It's great your dad helped you—but there's something else going on. And whatever it is, it's bigger than Jim."

"What do you mean? Something going on about what?"

"Mr. Healy's murder. Last night Junie came into my room and said, 'If people don't stop asking questions, someone's going to get hurt.' I asked him what he meant and who would be involved, but he refused to answer. When I kept asking, he walked out and slammed the door. But he made it sound like there's a reason for Jim to be afraid."

"I don't know, Shan. Jim told me the *evil ones* had tried to tear his raincoat. And then he thought that I'd gone over to their side."

"His paranoia could be based on real threats. You said the raincoat was messed up."

"He could have caught it on the fence or something."

"Maybe. . . ." Shan nods, but she doesn't look convinced. She folds a pair of T-shirts, sets them to one side. "Junie knows something, but he's afraid to tell."

"What makes you think that?"

"I don't know, exactly. For a while I was furious at him for being so mean. But now I get the feeling that he's trapped. When he's mad, it's like someone who's struggling in a web that's wrapping tighter and tighter around him. Mom and Dad don't get it—they think it's normal teenage stuff."

"Did you ask him what he knows?"

"I didn't, but Jim did. Junie called him loco and told him to get lost."

"I bet a lot of people tell him that."

She nods, but she looks unhappy, like whatever's upsetting Junie is bothering her, too.

= = = = = = = = = = = = = =

Walking home, I avoid the alleys and stick to the main streets, where people can see me. There's hardly anyone on the corner or in front of the Starcraft Bar; only Mr. Tibby, with his pile of newspapers, and a few boys I don't know. A car pulls over, but it's just to buy the paper. My block is quiet, and our house seems silent and empty. I want to feel lighthearted, but something's pulling me back. *"Like someone struggling in a web that's wrapping tighter and tighter around him,"* Shan had said. And then I hear Jim's voice: *"Jerry and I are the only ones left. . . ."*

I feel trapped, too. That makes me think of Jess inside her cage. I don't even know if she's alive.

I decide to pray. At school they encourage us to say our prayers, but at home I usually feel like I've got other things to do. Today is different. I say a couple Hail Marys, then three Our Fathers. The words and rhythms are peaceful. My parents say their prayers before they go to bed. I told Shannon that, and she said it was nice. I asked her, "Don't you believe in God a tiny bit?"

"No."

"Why not?"

She shrugged. *"I never have."*

"Who made the world, then?"

"I heard it got formed from an explosion of gases in outer space."

"But look at flowers and butterflies . . . look at that cardinal, sitting on the branch in the backyard. How could that come from smoke and flames?"

"I'm not sure. . . ."

"People are religious all over the world."

"What they believe doesn't change the way I feel."

= = = = = = = = = = = = = = =

I take Bobo with me when I pick up Jerry. Mrs. Brill looks nervous, 'cause the kids crowd around him, trying to pat his head. Jerry shows off, kissing Bobo on the nose. He takes the leash from me and walks him home. "Giddy-up, trot, walk," he shouts. Bobo just ignores him.

Nineteen

The next morning I leave Jerry at day care, then drop by Dollar Discount on my way to the Laundromat. For a moment I just stand there, staring. Jess's cage is empty.

My throat feels all dried up. "What happened?" I ask the clerk.

"What happened to what?"

"Jess— The canary that was in this cage."

The gray-haired woman shrugs. "It was sick. I think maybe it died."

"Where did they put her?"

"In the Dumpster. They can't leave dead animals inside the store." Then she sees I'm upset.

"Listen, hon, they could have sold her. That happens. In fact, maybe they told me that they did."

I know she's trying to be nice. I can't believe I'll never

hear her song again. I wipe my eyes and swallow, push my feelings deep inside.

= = = = = = = = = = = = = =

I help Shan at the Laundromat. She's sad about Jess, too. "You really loved that bird," she says. We sit across the table, matching pairs of socks. It helps to have something else to focus on. "Are you still talking to that boy?" I ask.

"Yes. He calls me every night."

"That's nice." I feel worse. Shan probably senses that.

"He's sweet, but he may not be my type."

"How come?"

She shrugs, like maybe she's not sure.

"It's cool you have a boyfriend."

"He's not, really—we've never been on a date."

"Did he ask you?"

"Yes, but my folks won't let me go. They say I can invite him to supper, but I don't want to. We have too many arguments these days."

"Invite him on a night when Junie won't be there."

"He's grounded."

"For what?"

"Sneaking out of the house, losing Daddy's cell phone . . . the list goes on and on."

The socks are done. Mr. Louras thanks Shan and gives her ten dollars. Then we head for McDonald's.

= = = = = = = = = = = = = = =

As usual, it's a big drama, today starring the fry cook and the girl that sweeps the outside walks. Shan's friend Ray comes partway through our time. He's real polite: "Am I interrupting?" Shan lights up when he's around. They talk about why they want to go to medical school and which is better, a psychiatrist or a surgeon, which is what he wants to be. They ask me what I think. What I think is: I can't believe they found each other at McDonald's.

They say that on the day I wasn't there, Shan was reading a book about a doctor, *Helping Hands.* Ray noticed her because he'd read it, too. He asked if he could sit with her to talk about the book, and that's how they got started. *Helping Hands* was required reading back in fifth grade at Saint Mary's, but I don't say that.

Ray has a summer job at City Hospital, delivering mail. Today he leaves at noon to catch the bus. "He's nice," I tell Shan. She grins all over her face.

We head back home. We don't walk through the alley, and we don't see Jim.

We go together to get Jerry. Then, on the spur of the moment, we walk to Baskin-Robbins for ice cream. Jerry gets so covered with chocolate that he looks half human and half monster. We rinse him with the hose. Then he cries because his clothes are wet. "Big baby," I tease, but Shan goes upstairs to his room and gets shorts and a T-shirt so he'll shut up. Later we let Bobo off his chain and squirt him, too. He runs around and tries to grab the stream of water with his mouth. Naturally Jerry thinks that's hilarious.

After a while Marcus rides up on his bike. When he sees us laughing, he knows that something's changed.

"What happened?"

"I'll tell you later."

He nods, grabs the hose, and turns on us. Jerry's jumping up and down, clapping his hands. I dodge in front of Marcus, and Shan sneaks behind and pulls the hose out of his hands. Jerry screams and starts running. Marcus lets us squirt him all we want. Then Jerry comes back and lets us squirt him, too.

We can't go in the house because we're drenched. Finally we strip Jerry to his underwear and send him in for towels. He comes back with an armful. A minute later Mom gets home.

"Charlie, what's going on?"

"We're drying off."

"I see that—" She looks around and sees the puddles, our wet hair. Then she smiles at us and goes on in the house. She doesn't even mention the pile of soaking-wet towels.

Twenty

This goes on for two more days: summer like it should be. I try not to think of Jess, or of Shan's warning: *"It's bigger than Jim."* Instead we sit on Mr. Healy's front porch and wish he could be there. "Do you remember?" Marcus asks, and then we talk about the games and the stories and the ice cream and the nights we sat here listening to the ball game on the radio. For years we were the same group: Uncle Mac, Shan, Junie, Marcus, Jerry, and me. When he was little, Kyle used to come and sometimes bring Jay-Jay. Now and then, Ms. Essie dropped by, or one of the other neighbors, taking an evening stroll, would stop on the sidewalk and listen to what was going on. Shan's remembering, too. "What will be left of him, once they sell this house?" she asks. There isn't even a gravestone to visit, because his son took the little box of ashes home to California.

Jerry has a funeral for him anyway, like he does for everything that dies: bugs and frogs and mice, even a gross old rat that got run over on the next block down. (Jerry cried over the stinky thing till Dad went down there with a shovel, scraped it off the street, and brought it home.) Jerry made it a casket out of a shoe box and buried it in the backyard. He prayed over it by himself, because I refused to go to a rat's funeral. Then he made a cross out of Popsicle sticks, printed *rat* across the top, and stuck it in the dirt. Mom says Shannon and I can't step on those crosses, even though we've got a burial ground full of them back there. "What if we want to play volleyball?"

"Use Mr. Healy's yard," she always says.

= = = = = = = = = = = = = =

With Jerry, you just never know. The next day Shan and I are at McDonald's, eating fries, when his day-care group files by. Jerry sees us, puts his face against the glass, and makes pop eyes. I yell at him to go away. Mrs. Brill takes his hand and leads him off. "Good riddance!" Shan only laughs, because Jerry's goofing never bothers her.

She tells me more about Ray, who didn't come because he had to be at work at ten. He has six brothers and one sister, and his dad works for CSX, the railroad line that brings in freight. His mom is a nurse on the maternity ward at Hopkins. "She started introducing him to doctors when he was four. They'd talk to him and take him to the doctors' lounge for snacks. By the time he started school, he knew he wanted to be a surgeon."

She hesitates. "We're different that way. I never wanted to cut people open—it's too bloody."

"Then why are you saving for medical school?"

"Remember how I told you that they think messed-up chemicals inside your brain can make you crazy? To prescribe medicine for that, you have to be a doctor."

"How come?"

"I'm not exactly sure."

= = = = = = = = = = = = = =

After I pick up Jerry, we head to Uncle Mac's. Jerry hasn't been there in almost a week, and he's yanking my arm so hard it feels like he may pull it off.

"Hurry up, Charlie . . . come on, hurry!"

"You don't when I want *you* to go somewhere."

"I do. Sometimes." He says it softly.

"Jerry, I'm not running in this heat."

"Is it hot?" He stops for a minute, like he needs to feel the air to know it's true.

"It's ninety-seven degrees, and that's probably in the shade!"

"Ninety-seven," he mumbles. I swear to you, Jerry is not of this world. "Mrs. Brill was sweating, too."

"Where did you kids go?"

"To the library. We each picked out a book, but I finished mine before we left, so I gave it back to them."

"What was it?"

"Momo the Monkey."

"Jerry, you have that at home! And it's a baby book!"

He studies the sidewalk ahead of him. "So?"

"So, the point of going there is to get something you don't already have!"

"Momo's my favorite."

"It's got about ten words in it." I know it by heart from reading it to him when he was small. "You can read anything. Why would you pick a silly book like that?" I start reciting it. " 'This is Momo. Momo is a monkey. He plays at the zoo.' "

"Shut up, Charlie." He stops abruptly, arms crossed. When I see beyond his glasses to his eyes, I realize he's upset. I wait for a minute, hoping he'll come out of it.

"Come on, Jerr . . . you want to see Uncle Mac, don't you?"

"I'm not going with you. You're too mean!" And suddenly he just takes off.

= = = = = = = = = = = = = =

He's scrawny, but he's fast. He darts behind a brick duplex and hightails it up the alley. I run behind him, but I can't keep up because he got the jump on me.

"Jerry! Come back here! Come back here right now!"

No answer.

"Jerry, where are you?"

No answer.

"JERRY!"

I trudge up the alley. Then I start trotting, calling Jerry. I go back to the sidewalk on the street and look for him. I'm furious. Maybe I shouldn't have teased him, but running away is totally irresponsible. Should I go home and hope that he'll turn up? Wait for him at the intersection where we'd cross the street to go to Uncle Mac's? Or could he have crossed it on his own?

= = = = = = = = = = = = = =

Today a crowd is hanging out. Some are waiting for the bus; others wander in and out of the bar or lounge around. Kyle nods at me from where he's leaning against the wall, but his eyes look blank, like nobody's home inside his head. Mr. Tibby's got his stack of newspapers. He smiles when I approach.

"How do, little sister?"

"Not too good. Jerry got mad at me and took off through the alley. I thought he might have come down here to cross the street."

"I haven't seen Jerry. Most everybody's in their house, with all this smog and heat."

"It doesn't bother him, because he's little."

"It sure does bother me."

Mr. Tibby's girlfriend, Rhonda, is sitting on the public bench. She holds a paper cup to her forehead. I guess there's ice inside. "What should we say if we see him?"

"Tell him to go home."

"I will." She nods, but I trust Mr. Tibby more, because she's got one foot in the Starcraft Bar before I turn around.

= = = = = = = = = = = = = =

I head back up the block. I'm not as far as Ms. Essie's before Marcus comes shooting past on his bike. I wave him down.

"Have you seen Jerry?"

"Not today."

"Could you help look for him? He got mad at me and ran away."

"Where to?"

"He took off down the alley."

Marcus turns his bike around and sails away.

"I'll be at home," I shout after him. "If you find Jerry, bring him there."

= = = = = = = = = = = = = =

I'm hoping he'll be waiting on the porch, but he's not. I unlock the door, calling "Jerry!" Then I check every room, even the closets. Jerry can be strange when he's upset.

He's not here. I'm really getting scared. Shan's line is busy, so I leave a message. I'm about to call Mom when I look out the kitchen window and see Jerry sitting beside Bobo in the doghouse.

I go out back. Bobo jumps up and starts wagging his tail, but Jerry stays put. "Hey," I say, "you got me scared."

He looks at me and doesn't answer. His face is even paler than usual.

"You shouldn't run away like that," I go on. "I've been looking all over for you."

Nothing.

"Are you still mad about the monkey book?"

He nods.

"I'm sorry I said that, okay? I mean, it wasn't to hurt your feelings. It just happens to be my opinion of that book."

He doesn't answer. He looks like he's been slapped.

"Okay, Jerry, come inside. You can bring Bobo with you. Find the book, and I'll read it to you like I used to."

He does get up then, even though he isn't smiling, and comes in, with Bobo behind him.

= = = = = = = = = = = = = =

I get in the rocking chair and let him sit in my lap. My mind is screaming, "You're seven years old!" but I keep my mouth shut and read the stupid book out loud. Jerry sucks his thumb, lets one foot drag on the floor while we're rocking back and forth. I read the last sentence: "'And Momo was the happiest monkey in the whole wide world.'" When I close the book, Jerry starts crying.

"What's wrong? Are your feelings still hurt?"

He burrows down against me, like a frightened rabbit.

"Did something happen?"

He stays in the same position.

"Are you still mad at me?"

He shakes his head no.

Just then the doorbell rings. Marcus doesn't wait for us to let him in. We hear his voice floating up from the living room. "Did you find him, Charlie?"

"Yeah, he's up here."

I guess Jerry doesn't want Marcus to think he's a baby, because he wipes his eyes and jumps off my lap. A minute later, Marcus is standing in the doorway.

"Where you been, dude? I was looking for you."

"Here."

"You run straight back home?"

Jerry nods.

"Whew." Marcus wipes his round, shiny face with the edge of his T-shirt. "You got me overheated. Hope y'all have some soda downstairs."

"We do," I tell Marcus. "I'll get you one."

"Me, too," Jerry cries. "I want one, too."

He sounds normal, so as I head for the kitchen, I'm smiling.

= = = = = = = = = = = = = =

Shannon comes a minute later. When she hears Jerry's found, she's relieved.

"I was afraid we were going to have to look in that filthy gas station. Imagine what it smells like in all this heat." She makes a face. Shan likes things clean and sweet-smelling, like fresh sheets. "Why did Jerry run off, anyway?"

"We had an argument, and I guess I hurt his feelings." I give her the details.

She smiles. "You probably had some favorite baby book."

"Maybe." The truth is, Mom read me *The Poky Little Puppy* till the cover fell off. Then I cried, and she glued it back again. I'd forgotten about that.

"I probably shouldn't have teased him. But *Momo the Monkey* is such a wimpy book."

"He's okay now?"

"Yeah, he's playing with Marcus. I hope he doesn't tell on me."

"Me, too." Shan nods, but she looks preoccupied. "I need to talk to you."

We go up to my room and lie down on my bed. Shan tugs

at the pillow, folds it back behind her head. "Ray invited me over to meet his family Sunday afternoon. Only"—she bites her lip—"I'm not sure I want to go."

"How come?"

"They're real religious. What if they ask me where I go to church?"

It takes me a minute to grasp her dilemma. "Say you don't."

"Don't you think they'll ask me why?"

"It's not their business."

"What if you were dating someone? Wouldn't your parents want to know?"

The fact is, they would. And since Shan almost always tells the truth, even when I don't want to hear it, I nod. "Probably."

"Would they stop you dating someone who wasn't Catholic?"

"I don't think so."

"What if he was Jewish?"

"My dad's got Jewish friends. And Mom likes everyone."

"What if he was an atheist?"

"Uhhh . . . I'm not sure. They like you," I point out.

"They probably don't know. Did you ever tell them?"

"No."

"See what I mean?"

I shrug. "Did you tell Ray?"

"No, because he hasn't asked. But when he does, I will."

"You really like him, huh?"

She nods. Her face looks different, older and kind of sparkly. I realize suddenly—hugely—that Shan's in love.

= = = = = = = = = = = = = =

That night I test Shan's situation on my folks. I wait until we've started eating and the usual questions—What did you do today?—are over. Then I ask straight out, "Would you mind if I married an atheist?"

My dad chokes on a mouthful of fried fish. Mom sits up and scowls at me because she knows that this is trouble. Jerry whispers, "What's an atheist?"

"Somebody who doesn't believe in God."

"Why not?"

"They just don't think he's there."

"Did someone tell them that?"

"Maybe." I answer his questions because my folks seem tongue-tied. "Or maybe they just got that idea on their own."

"Do you believe that, Charlie?"

"Of course not. How could I go to Saint Mary's if I didn't believe in God?"

"You could lie, and do it anyway."

"Wait a minute here!" Dad's got his breath back now, and I can tell that he's upset. "How did *this* get started?"

"Shan said something about it."

"About marrying an atheist? I didn't know she was engaged."

"She's got a boyfriend," Jerry says. "I saw them holding hands."

"And he's an atheist? I'm glad that's Leo and Karen's problem, instead of mine."

I don't say anything, so I'm not lying.

Mom says, "I thought she wanted to go to medical school."

"She does, and he does, too."

"Then they'll both be doctors," Jerry says.

Mom nods. Then she notices Jerry's plate. "Why aren't you eating? I made that macaroni just for you."

"I'm not hungry."

"Are you sick?"

Jerry shakes his head, but he does look pale.

She feels his forehead. "You're clammy. Are you sure you feel okay?"

"Yes."

"Did something happen?" She looks at me sharply, then at him.

"I didn't mean to, but—"

"No," Jerry says forcefully. He shoots me a look that says *shut up.*

"What did you eat at Mrs. Brill's?"

"Grilled cheese and applesauce—and a Popsicle for snack."

Mom sighs. "If you feel okay and you don't eat your dinner, it's straight to bed with no TV."

"Can I go now?"

"Yes. I'll be up to see you in a little while."

= = = = = = = = = = = = = =

Of course I'm suspect number one, even though they don't have the faintest idea what happened. Dad says, "No more talk about atheists. You got Jerry so upset that he can't eat."

"You don't know it was that."

"What was it, then?"

If I tell the truth they'll say, We knew it was your fault. So I shrug. "I'm not sure. He seemed upset after day care, but later he cheered up."

= = = = = = = = = = = = = =

I go to bed feeling worried. And sometime in the middle of that night, I wake up and hear the rocker going—*squeak, squeak, squeak.*

Twenty-one

"**J**esus died to save us," Jerry says while I'm pouring his Cheerios. "Isn't that right, Charlie?"

"Of course. You go to church, same as me."

"Because of our sins, right?"

"I guess."

"Like lying, or hurting people or animals."

I don't say anything.

"I don't want to hurt things, Charlie. Even plants." He looks down at his cereal. "These oats were alive, you know? They were growing—"

"Jerry, please!"

"Killing is evil, Charlie. Once you kill something, it's gone forever."

"Everything dies eventually. That's the way the world's

set up. You said it yourself—if they didn't, it would get too crowded."

"Dead things take up space."

"Until they rot."

"They don't rot. They're all there, in the cemeteries."

"What about someone like Mr. Healy? He had his body burned, so he was only ashes."

"Someone killed him. Did you know that, Charlie?"

"I . . . Who told you that?"

"I found out the truth." He looks at me accusingly.

"I would have told you, but Mom and Dad said not to."

"Liar."

"Not—they were afraid you'd be upset."

"And so you lied."

He won't talk to me after that, and all he'll drink is a glass of milk, since nothing died to make it.

"This is so crazy! Mom and Dad are going to flip out! And what will you do at Mrs. Brill's?"

He doesn't answer, and on the way to day care, he refuses to hold my hand.

≡ ≡ ≡ ≡ ≡ ≡ ≡ ≡ ≡ ≡ ≡ ≡ ≡ ≡

Shan is sweating over a pile of sheets. She's glad to see me, because "these are impossible for me to fold by myself." I stand away and we two-step toward each other, flip the fabric, do the same again. After they're done, we sit back down. She hands me socks to tuck inside each other. "Be careful—they're Mr. Molloy's. If we lose one, we'll be back at the Large and Tall." We laugh, remembering the skinny little clerk with his nose up in the air. Then Shan says, "I told Junie about Ray."

"What did he say?"

"If his family's open-minded, they'll accept you. If they aren't, you probably don't want to know them anyway."

"That's a good answer."

"I thought so. But Junie doesn't agree with my atheism, either. He said there has to be a God, so people can have hope."

"What do your parents think?"

She laughs. "They're still trying to get me back in church, especially Dad. He thinks everyone needs Jesus. But he won't force me. Maybe he understands it wouldn't do any good."

I tell Shannon about Jerry. "He found out the truth about Mr. Healy, so he's all shook up. Now he doesn't want anything to be killed, not even plants. And he's mad at me for lying to him."

"Your parents told you to."

"I said that, but it didn't make any difference."

Shan's folding the last things in the bin. "He's going to be angry at them, too."

= = = = = = = = = = = = =

We walk to McDonald's. This is the second day that Ray's had to leave for work early, so it feels like old times. We talk about TV and bands and the clothes we want from the fashion magazines. Shan likes black-dress sophisticate, with lots of diamonds; I'll go for the gypsy look, with my hair long and loose. If I were a model, I'd want my picture taken with a cowboy and a horse. Shan laughs. She'd be in a nightclub, lolling against a velvet drape. "By day I'll be a doctor; by night, a fashion queen."

I think of Jim. *"By day they're innocent. By night they're something else."*

"I've almost got it solved," he'd said that evening in the alley. Had he really figured out who killed Mr. Healy?

= = = = = = = = = = = = = =

We go to Shan's. Junie's stretched out on the living-room couch in boxers and a T-shirt. Before I can say hi, he starts fussing at me. "Aren't you supposed to be taking care of Jerry?"

"I am taking care of him."

"Then you need to do a better job of it."

"What are you talking about?"

"I saw him talking to that crazy dude."

"You mean the raincoat man?"

He nods.

"When?"

"One morning last week, around seven. He was in your side yard, and Jerry was leaning out his bedroom window."

At first I just stand there with my mouth open. "That's not true! I would have heard them!"

"You think I'd make it up?"

"Jerry was asleep! I'm the one who wakes him up!"

He shrugs. "Have it your way, Charlie. But let me give you one word of advice—"

"Don't talk down to me, Junie!"

He looks surprised. "I didn't think I was."

There's a silence between us, a silence where some barrier is eased in a way that I don't understand. "What were you going to say?" I murmur.

"That you and Jerry should keep away from the raincoat man. His talk will lead to trouble."

"He's just asking questions. That's not against the law."

"The law has nothing to do with us. We grew up sheltered, Charlie. Eventually you'll find out the truth. On these streets, it's dog-eat-dog."

He heads down the hall. A second later his door slams shut.

= = = = = = = = = = = = = =

I take Jerry to Uncle Mac's. That's my best bet for getting him relaxed. Otherwise, when I start the questions, he'll clam up. Mr. Tibby's standing at the intersection with his papers. "So you found him." He pats Jerry on the head. "We miss you when you're gone," he says.

= = = = = = = = = = = = = =

Uncle Mac's in a good mood. He's bent over a truck engine, whistling. Jerry stands beside him, asking questions. I sit on the workbench.

"How can you tell the hose is worn?"

"Just look at it. See how it's frayed around the edges?"

"Can I have it?"

"Sure."

Jerry's in heaven. In the meantime, cats are everywhere. They start crowding up against me, purring and rubbing. I push them away, because they make me hot. Now they're under the truck, yowling. Maybe they know when Jerry comes, they're going to get fed.

Finally Uncle Mac gives in: "Let's get them some milk. Then we'll come back and close the door."

Jerry leads the cats into the office, with Uncle Mac behind. While they're out there, I get a Coke from the machine and look under the hood myself. I don't know as much as Jerry, but I do know some, because Dad taught us the parts of the engine. He says it's a manmade miracle when a motor works just right, and a half cup of gas will run a two-ton truck. Jerry wants to be a mechanic like Uncle Mac, but he also wants to save animals from extinction and be a baseball star and an explorer.

Now they're back, the two of them smiling and Jerry even swaggering a little, like he does when he's just totally happy. He stays that way until we leave. But after we cross the boulevard, I repeat what Junie said. Jerry swears up and down it isn't true. A minute later, glancing up Lanvale Street, I see Jim ahead of us. I stop dead. Jerry looks up and sees him, too.

"He's different than we thought," he says. "When he's finished what he's doing, there won't be any more killing. The old world will disappear, and the new one will be perfect, like it was in the beginning—"

"Did he tell you that?"

Jerry nods. He's almost glowing. "We'll have to make some sacrifices now, but later, it will all be great."

I can't help myself, I just freak out. "You're not supposed to talk to Jim! Don't you know that he's a nut?"

"He's not."

"Jerry, you can't trust Jim. He's telling lies!"

"You and Mom and Dad are the liars," Jerry says.

"I told you, they thought you'd be upset!"

Jerry stops and crosses his arms in front of him. His voice is defiant. "You don't see the evil that's around us.

What happened to Mr. Healy's just a part of it. People and animals and plants are being killed every single second, and it could be stopped."

"How?"

Jerry won't answer.

I grab his shoulders. "Tell!"

"Owwww. . . ." His thin bones wriggle underneath my grip. "You're hurting me!" he cries.

"You have to tell me what's going on!"

"I can't!"

"Why not?"

"Because I'll ruin it!" He starts crying, but he won't say anything more.

= = = = = = = = = = = = = =

"Jerry found out how Mr. Healy died," I say to Mom when we're alone. "And now he's mad at us, because we lied."

Mom calls Mrs. Brill. It turns out one of the little kids told the others what happened. When Dad comes in, Mom speaks to him upstairs. Supper's strained, and afterward the two of them take Jerry on a walk to Baskin-Robbins. I guess they're trying to straighten things out, but whatever they say to each other, they leave me in the dark when they come back.

= = = = = = = = = = = = = =

Next morning Jerry doesn't say a word about yesterday. He eats his cereal and slurps the milk out of the bowl. After I drop him off, I head straight to the Laundromat. I tell Shan about the "sacrifices."

"What do you think Jim's talking about?"

"Somebody needs to find that out."

Hair stands up on the back of my neck. I look over at Shan, to see if she notices that I'm afraid.

But she has news, too. Last night there was a raid down on the boulevard. The police took fifteen people, even Mr. Tibby. Ms. Essie went this morning to ask for his release.

"Who else did they get?"

"Bitty and Kyle. Junie says they're in the East Side Brokers now. The boss is a Jamaican who runs crack down from New York."

A shiver inches down my spine. "I can't believe Kyle's part of that."

Shan shrugs. "Junie says Jay-Jay's with them, too, and I think he's right." She nods toward the back of the Laundromat. "Last week I was in the storeroom searching for detergent. I looked out the big window and saw Jay-Jay counting money and sticking it in his shoes."

"Kids at school used to say that he was really dumb."

"If he's in that gang, they're right." Shan sighs. "Sometimes I can't wait to get out of here," she says.

= = = = = = = = = = = = =

When we get to McDonald's, Ray's already there. He buys us sodas and extra fries. He's nice: "How ya doing, Charlie? Shan said if I called you Charlene, I'd get smacked."

"That's right." It's hard not to smile at him. When he smiles back, I see what Shannon likes. His eyes are deep but friendly and make you feel calm.

= = = = = = = = = = = = = = =

After he leaves to go to work, I ask Shan to come to Dollar Discount. At first she doesn't want to.

"Why upset yourself?" she asks.

"Maybe she's back."

"You know she's not."

"I want to look there, just in case." Hearing Jess made me feel still inside, like I was sitting in the woods beside a silver pond.

"Charlie. . . ." Shan shakes her head.

"Please?"

She can't say no to that.

= = = = = = = = = = = = = = =

There is a new canary in the cage, but it's a different shade of yellow and smaller. It stares at me, then turns away. A clerk sees me hanging around the birdcages. She's different from the last one I talked to—narrow-shouldered and mousy.

"Ain't you that girl that always came in here?"

"I guess."

"Wasn't there a bird you liked—you and your little brother?"

I nod.

"I sold that bird." She seems excited. "I thought of you, 'cause I expected you was going to buy it. But somebody beat you to it."

"Who?"

"A big black man, walks with a cane. I don't know his name, but you can't miss him. He must weigh three hundred, maybe more."

"Thanks."

"He beat you to it," she says again, like she thinks she's hurting me. "Guess you spent so much time looking that you didn't get your money together fast enough."

"Let's leave," Shan says. "She's getting on my nerves."

The clerk takes offense at that, of course. She has no idea what good news she just gave me, and I don't let her find out.

Twenty-two

Shan's surprised that I don't go to the Molloys' right then. But I have to find out what Jerry meant about the sacrifices, and if I don't do it now, I'll lose my nerve. I take a deep breath.

"I've got work to do in the backyard—mowing and pulling weeds along the fence. Want to come?"

I know she'll refuse. Shan isn't a nature lover. Sometimes she says she'd rather stay indoors for the rest of her life. She doesn't even want a cat or dog, because they're too smelly. Wonder if she's said *that* to Ray.

= = = = = = = = = = = = = = =

I check the alley up and down, and then the one behind the next street over. Mr. Tibby's back on the corner. I don't ask about his time in jail.

"You mean the raincoat man? I saw him on the sidewalk by the city yard last night."

= = = = = = = = = = = = = = =

The morgue runs past the city yard and out the other side, around the railroad tracks. It's overgrown and trashy. There's trees sprouting up like weeds and old mattresses and broken glass. Vines cling to everything, as if it all belongs to them. Rats crisscross the underbrush, scuttling back and forth. It's a place to dump dead bodies—shot or stabbed or beaten up. The police don't ask who did it, because they don't want to go in there themselves. I'm scared 'cause people say that homeless men sleep in the brush on summer nights; drunks and crackheads, too.

I look for Jim. Nothing. But to my right, I hear movements in the brush. Then voices: "Over here again . . . didn't send the . . . he was supposed to . . ."

"Man, I don't know . . ."

The voices rise and fall, like bad reception on a cell phone. Then mumbling. Voices back. One of them is vaguely familiar.

". . . If he doesn't keep the agreement . . ."

"I told you, man, we're doing . . ."

"I told *you* . . ."

There's a sound behind me. I whirl and see Jim. He must have come while I was eavesdropping. He puts one finger to his lips, gestures for me to follow him. I shake my head no. He grabs my arm.

"Let me go!"

"Don't you understand? It's dangerous!" His eyes sweep toward the place the voices come from. He pulls at me to cross the street. Once we get there, he takes the little notebook from his pocket and starts scribbling. When he's done, he asks, "What in the world are you doing here?"

"Looking for you."

"Your father asked me not to talk to you!"

"I know, but Jerry told me what you said . . ."

He waits.

". . . About going back to the Garden of Eden, all that stuff. He said there will be sacrifices. . . ."

He nods.

"I don't want anything to happen to Jerry!"

He stares at me like I'm an idiot. "Nothing will happen to Jerry. I told you over and over, he's special."

"Why do you keep saying that?"

"You haven't figured it out?"

"What?"

"*A little child shall lead them . . .*"

I can't remember where that's from. The rumble of a train begins far off in the distance. Its passengers look out the windows at green yards, new houses. The track sounds like it's singing one long, high, shivery note.

"Don't worry," he tells me then. "It won't be like Jesus. This time it's going to turn out well." He acts like he's talking about something everyone knows but me. "The final battle is approaching. There will be fires and floods and lightning, but on Judgment Day, God will triumph. Then the truth will be revealed—who killed Mr. Healy and the other sins, too."

I take a step back. "You're crazy," I say softly.

"I know." Jim is matter-of-fact. "Pretty soon I'll be back in the hospital. But once I am, you'll still find out I'm right."

"Right about what?"

"About the Judgment Day. The killers are going to prison. I found the witnesses to back me up."

"What are you talking about?"

His voice drops. "I saw the ones who did it."

"When?"

"The night when he was killed." His words come in a frenzy. "I was watching *The Late Show* when I heard a noise. I got up, opened my bedroom door, and listened. There were voices. I crept down a step or two and saw Mr. Healy standing in the doorway. He was arguing with someone. After that came something sharp—*pop, pop.* I was so scared, I ran back to my room. When I looked out the window, I saw three people run across the yard and down the street."

Jim's sniffling now. "I hoped it was a delusion—you

know, paranoia. Maybe I'd take my pills and wait awhile and go downstairs, and he'd be sitting in his rocking chair or asleep in front of the TV. I sat up on my bed all night, scared to find out what had happened. When the ambulance arrived, I knew that he was dead." Tears streak Jim's face. "I should have gone to help him. He helped me. When I got out of the hospital, nobody else would take me in."

He chokes back sobs. "But I saw them. And there were others who did, too. That's why I'm writing down what people witnessed in their own words—"

"You mean there were others besides you?"

"People heard and saw things, but they were scared to tell."

"Then why'd they talk to you?"

"Maybe they felt guilty. It's hard to keep a secret like that."

I stand there letting his words sink in. I feel drained.

"But who was it? Who did you see?"

He doesn't answer me. He whispers:

The wolf also shall dwell with the lamb, and the leopard shall lie down with the kid; and the calf and the young lion and the fatling together; and a little child shall lead them. . . . They shall not hurt nor destroy in all my holy mountain: for the earth shall be full of the knowledge of the Lord, as the waters cover the sea.

Jim's in his own world. When he notices that I'm still here, he acts like we were having a completely different conversation. "Don't go back into those woods," he says. He gestures toward the morgue. "There are people in there who will do you harm."

Twenty-three

I pick Jerry up from day care. There on the sidewalk in front of Mrs. Brill's, I tell him what Jim said.

"You know he's crazy, don't you?" I ask.

"No, I think he's right."

"About what?"

"About being honest instead of lying and letting people and animals be murdered and trying to get justice. . . ." He blinks at me behind his owlish glasses. "He knows who did it. Now he's backing up the evidence. On the right day, he'll give everything to the police."

"The Day of Judgment?"

He nods solemnly.

"The day you're going to save the world?" Sarcasm creeps into my question. Jerry doesn't notice how I feel.

"I'm not going to save the world," he says. Tears well up in his eyes. "I want to, but I don't know how."

= = = = = = = = = = = = = =

The rest of the afternoon I keep Jerry busy playing Nintendo, brushing Bobo, playing checkers with Marcus on the front porch. When Mom comes home, I start to tell her what Jim said. But the minute she hears that I went looking for the raincoat man, her eyes flash. "Charlie!"

"I had to! I thought Jerry was going to get hurt!"

Her mouth is set in a straight line. "Go on."

"Jim's really loco, Mom. He thinks Jerry has been picked by God to lead us, and there's going to be a judgment day, and afterward the world will be like heaven. He says he saw the killers, too. . . ."

"There's no excuse whatsoever for you going down beside the yard looking for that man! And going by the train tracks!"

"Stop thinking about me! Focus on what he's saying!"

"What he's saying is crazy, but he isn't hurting anyone! You've been told over and over again to stay away from him!"

= = = = = = = = = = = = = =

When Dad gets home, Mom calls him into the kitchen. I don't know exactly what she says, but he comes out fuming. "I've had it!" he yells. "Jerry's never seeing Jim Chalmers again, and neither are you, Charlie, because I'm calling the police on him right now!"

At first Jerry doesn't get it. "To tell them about the investigation?"

"*What* investigation?" Then Dad remembers. "Oh, this has nothing to do with that. He shouldn't even be talking to you kids. I warned him, and he did it anyway."

"You warned him about *Charlie!*" Jerry yelps. "Not me! Anyway, Charlie went looking for him, so it's not his fault."

"He's putting weird ideas into your head. I think he's dangerous, and I'm calling the police."

"Dad, NO!" Jerry starts shrieking. He falls down on the floor, writhing like he's been shot.

Dad doesn't like loud noises, because they remind him of the war.

"Jerry, be quiet," he says. Of course, my brother pays no attention. Finally Dad loses it and yells, "JERRY, SHUT UP!"

For a second Jerry freezes. Then he begins to sob. Bobo didn't mind the screams, but when he hears this new sound, he sits down beside Jerry and starts to bark.

Dad throws his hands up. He kicks his work boots into a corner and stomps upstairs to take a shower.

Mom's still mad at me. "You have just about driven me nuts this summer," she says. "I'd like to lock you in your room until it's time for school to start."

= = = = = = = = = = = = = = =

Jerry cries a marathon. It doesn't matter that Marcus comes in and stares at him, or Bobo keeps barking, or Mom offers him ice cream. An hour's passed, but he hasn't let up. He won't even turn his head and look at us.

Finally Dad comes downstairs, picks him up, and sets him on the couch. Before Jerry can slither down into a spineless lump, he grabs Jerry's shoulders.

"What do you *want*?" he asks.

"I want you to believe him."

"All the screaming in the world isn't going to make me believe him, Jerry. As far as you being the next Jesus or Buddha or Muhammad, that's insane. The sooner you get that idea out of your head, the better."

Jerry starts crying all over again. He cries so hard that his whole body is heaving. Dad wants to pick him up and put him in his room, but Mom says no.

"You know Jerry. He won't eat or sleep until he has his say."

Maybe Jerry hears her, because he murmurs something through his sobs.

"What?" Mom asks.

"I . . . wan . . . to . . ." His voice is so hoarse, he has to whisper: "I want to see him one more time."

"No way!"

Jerry starts again. We could end up sitting here listening to him all night. Mom and Dad know it, too.

Dad's still angry. "You can write a note. Bring it here, and I'll take it to his house."

Jerry runs upstairs. A minute later he comes back down with a folded piece of paper in his hand. "I want to go, too. He's not there now. During the day, he's mostly in the alleys."

Dad's arms are crossed, but Mom's looking hard at him, so finally he agrees. "We'll take it," he says. "But I want to be perfectly clear. This is the last of you and Jim."

Jerry doesn't answer. "Come on, Charlie," he whispers. "You come, too."

Dad marches like he's back in the army. His lips are tight, and he's gripping Jerry's arm, pulling him along. I walk behind them, trying to keep up. When we get to the corner, Dad asks, "Which way?"

Jerry points south. Dad's surprised, because that part of the neighborhood's industrial. "Which street?"

"Right now he's living in the woods, 'cause he didn't have the money to pay rent. It's only for a little while," Jerry adds quickly.

"He lives inside the morgue? Did he take you there?"

"No, but he told me where to find his stuff, in case something happens to him."

"What would happen to him?"

Jerry and I glance at each other but say nothing.

= = = = = = = = = = = = = =

We get to the sidewalk where I heard the voices and saw Jim. "Farther," Jerry says. Down from that, a sign points toward the landfill. Jerry stops. "Here, I think."

We wade through honeysuckle and old bottles, pieces of cardboard, broken tree limbs. Dad's face is grim. "I don't see any sign—"

Jerry still checks his hands to tell left from right; the left one has a freckle on the thumb. "This way," he points. "Look for the thicket on the right." The morgue has more land than I realized. This could be a city park if they'd clean it up. Jerry worms his way forward. There's a wall of brush and vines in front of us. He scans it. "Here, maybe." He disappears into the thicket.

It turns out there's a little opening, almost invisible because of the high weeds. Inside, the morgue has been transformed. A circle of ground is cleared so you can see the earth. In the middle is a camp: blankets, a gallon jug of water, a shoe box tied with string, a Bible. There's a broken lawn chair that looks like it still works and a flashlight and a plastic envelope from a dry cleaner with folded shirts inside. Dad's stopped in his tracks.

"You're sure this stuff is his?"

"It's where he said . . ." Carefully Jerry opens the shoe box, which is stuffed with papers. Before he can leave the note on top, Dad takes the box away and rifles through the contents.

"Those are private!" Jerry cries.

"I know—I'll put it back." But I see Dad slip a letter into his pocket. He glances at some scraps of paper. "What's behind the Dollar Discount?" he asks. "That's written everywhere."

"I don't know." Jerry turns pale. But Dad must figure everything's under control, because he doesn't question Jerry further. He puts the shoe box back and sets Jerry's note on top. "You're sure he'll find it?"

Jerry nods.

"Poor guy—I would have brought him food if I'd known he was living down here."

"He's not poor."

"How come?"

"He's special, 'cause God spoke to him."

"Jerry . . ." Dad sighs. He looks up at the sky, like he's figuring out what to say. "You may be too young to understand, but people who think those thoughts are usually mentally ill."

"He's not." Jerry's jaw is set this certain way, like when he told me he was vegetarian.

Dad shrugs. "Have it your way. . . . I just don't want you to feel disappointed when you find out the truth."

Twenty-four

"**O**ne of the Chosen, huh?" Shan's sitting across from me at the Laundromat. She isn't as dismissive as I thought she'd be. "Jesus probably seemed strange to other people, too," she says.

"Of course he seemed different, because he was. He was God."

"How do you know Jerry isn't, too?"

"Because I know!" That's not a very good answer, and secretly I think maybe I'll ask Father Cronin about this. But in the meantime I go on. "Jim said he saw the murderers from his bedroom window—"

"What?" Shan's mouth is open, and her eyes get big. "Who are they?"

"He wouldn't say. But he claims other people saw them, too. That's why he was asking questions—to find more witnesses. Now he says he has enough to go to the police."

Shan's still staring at me. "They'll throw out the evidence, because he's mentally ill."

"He is, but I'm pretty sure that what he said about that night is true."

"Why didn't he tell you before?"

"I don't know. I think he was afraid."

She considers that. "He's right to be afraid. If the killers find out what he knows, they'll figure out a way to keep him quiet."

"I don't think they will find out, because he's leaving—he's going back into the hospital."

"He'll check himself in?"

"I'm not sure. If he doesn't, someone else may." I tell Shan about Dad taking the letter from the shoe box. "I think he's going to call Jim's mom."

"What would he say? Jim's a grown man."

"But if he's doing dangerous things—"

"That's still his business, isn't it?"

"What if his 'business' gets him or somebody else hurt?"

"You're thinking about Jerry?" She sighs. "Maybe you're right."

■ ■ ■ ■ ■ ■ ■ ■ ■ ■ ■ ■ ■ ■ ■

Before I pick up Jerry, I go to Uncle Mac's. He's bent over his lopsided metal desk, rummaging through papers. "Charlie," he murmurs absently. "What did I do with that muffler warranty?"

I don't answer. He sighs, then suddenly, under a messy stack, he finds it. "I thought so. . . . She's got a few months left. . . ." He folds the paper, puts it in the chest pocket of his coveralls. "No Jerry?"

"He's at day care."

He stands there, waiting.

"You know Jim, who used to live at Mr. Healy's?"

"The guy who wore the raincoat?"

"He might have seen who killed him."

He doesn't ask, Who did it? Instead he waits.

"He thinks other people might have seen them, too."

"I already told you, Charlie. I was here."

"You know so many people, because of their cars. . . . I thought somebody might have told you. . . ."

Uncle Mac coughs, like he's uncomfortable, and he doesn't meet my eyes. "Nobody needed to tell me. Arthur was always trying to get the dealers off that corner. He called the police."

"You mean that it was *them*?"

"I didn't see it happen." He's quiet suddenly. "And if I had, I wouldn't tell you, anyway."

The air around me has grown still. I'm hurt and furious at once, then scared. "Why not?"

He's stacking stuff back on his desk. The pile sways, and he has to grab it, take some off, and set it on his chair. Afterward, he turns and faces me.

"If they killed a man who reported they sold drugs, what do you think they'd do if someone claimed they were murderers?"

I just stand there.

"It's too dangerous for you to be involved in," he says brusquely. "Do what everybody else did. Go home and try to forget about it."

= = = = = = = = = = = = = = =

I sit in McDonald's by myself. Around me there's commotion: children crying, people laughing, teenagers emptying trash and wiping tables. I let myself breathe slowly in and out until my thoughts calm down. Did the dealers kill Mr. Healy? And were there people in the neighborhood who'd known it all along?

= = = = = = = = = = = = = = =

Jerry's poky when I pick him up. He scrapes his sneakers on the sidewalk, stares at every square of cement, as if it holds a mystery. We see bugs and caterpillars and a couple of earthworms, which Jerry transfers onto someone's lawn, "so they don't get squished." By the time we get home, Mom's already there. She makes me set the table and take out the trash.

Dad comes in tired and grumpy. Mom sticks his beer in the freezer, so it will be extra cold. She cautions me, *"Don't get into an argument with your dad tonight, Charlie. He was up late."*

"Doing what?"

"Now is not the time to tell you. . . ."

But maybe she doesn't warn Jerry, because as soon as we've said grace, he announces, "I told the other kids."

Mom's fork stops halfway to her mouth. "What kids?"

"The kids at Mrs. Brill's."

"What did you tell them?"

"About Jim and what he's trying to do."

Dad takes a deep breath. "I told you yesterday, Jim has mental problems."

"He does not! Jim's trying to save the world."

Dad turns red. "Jerry, *nobody* can save the world."

"You wanted to—you said that's why you went to war."

"I was young and stupid."

"Dom!" Mom glares at him.

"It's true!" Dad glares right back. "And they might as well know it. Daydreams are fine, but you need to understand exactly what they are: dreams. Otherwise, life will hand you a rude awakening."

"I'm not dreaming!" Jerry tells Dad. "The one who needs to wake up is you!"

For once he gets sent to his room before I do.

= = = = = = = = = = = = = =

I visit him later, bringing Bobo with me. Jerry gives him a great big kiss on his black nose. "You're my friend," Jerry tells him, "and not Dad." Then he asks, "Is Jim going to the hospital?"

"I don't know."

"Dad called someone last night. I heard him on the phone, talking about Jim."

"Who was he talking to?"

"I don't know, but he kept saying, 'He needs help.' He told the person where Jim's living, too."

"That's good. The morgue isn't safe."

"He doesn't have anyplace else!"

"There are shelters for homeless people."

"He said someone might steal his papers or his raincoat." Jerry's lying on his bed beside Bobo, looking at the ceiling. His fingers trace a crack that runs from the light to a spot above the window. "It's going to be soon," he says.

"Judgment Day? How do you know?"

He doesn't answer. "Was there dessert?"

"Only orange sherbet."

"I don't even like that . . . very much. . . ."

"I could probably sneak you some."

His eyes light up. "Now?"

"If Mom and Dad are watching TV . . ."

"Thanks." He snuggles up with Bobo.

When I come back with the bowl of sherbet, his thumb is in his mouth, and his eyes are already closed.

Twenty-five

Shan's in an awful mood. When I sit down, she's glaring at the clothes in front of her.

"What's wrong?"

"Junie." Her hands throw socks into the laundry cart like they're on fire. "Mom and Dad are *paying* for Junie to go to Chicago. You know how many times I've asked them—*begged* them—to send me there to visit Gramma and Grandpa and Uncle James, and they've always said they can't afford it and I'd have to pay my way. And now *he's* going!"

"When?"

"Next week!"

"Did they say why?"

"Something about special circumstances. . . . I asked *what* circumstances, and they wouldn't answer. And then they yelled at me for bugging them!"

I've seen Shan mad lots of times, but not like this.

"Plus," she adds, "I'm not supposed to tell."

"Why not?"

"Who knows?" She shrugs. "They told me not to tell until he left. I shouldn't have told you, but I had to. You're as much my family as they are."

"They said not to tell *me*?"

She nods. "Dad said, 'Don't breathe a word to anyone until he's gone—not even Charlie.' "

= = = = = = = = = = = = = =

I can't tell Jerry or Mom or Dad about Junie, since I'm not supposed to know. But they have a surprise for us, too, because after Mom gets home from work, kicks her shoes off, and sits down on the couch, she asks, "How would you like it if the four of us went bowling?"

"Tonight?"

"Yes, after Dad finishes his shower."

I'm too stunned to answer. There's never enough money in our house, so videos and ice cream are the usual treats. Jerry's as astounded as I am.

"How come?"

"We hardly ever go out together, and Dom and I've been thinking maybe we should."

They must be feeling guilty. Or maybe they think if they'd paid more attention, Jerry wouldn't have gotten involved with Jim or believed in his ideas. Even I know better than that.

= = = = = = = = = = = = = =

The evening's great. The heft of the ball and the splintering crack against the pins make me feel powerful. Mom and Dad enjoy themselves, too. He puts on a show, twisting and turning like a dancer, but she has better aim. They flirt with each other, Dad putting his arms around Mom's back to show her his technique. Jerry can hardly lift the ball. He staggers to the front of the lane, pushes it forward with both hands. Once he gets it going, the ball's weight keeps it rolling. He's happy if it hits a single pin.

Afterward we have pizza at Luigi's on Castle Street. They've delivered to us a couple times, but we've never gone to the restaurant to eat. It feels like someone's birthday. Jerry's not the least bit suspicious. All he talks about is cars: the latest models and how much they cost. Dad tells him which designs he thinks are good and which will fail. Mom and I sit there listening till the meal is done. Then we wander off to check out prices in the shoe store across the street. Later all four of us walk to Baskin-Robbins for ice cream. A pink and orange sunset stretches across the sky. It grows more and more vibrant, as if somewhere, over the horizon, the edge of the earth is on fire.

Twenty-six

Jerry blathers all the way to day care.

"I had a dream."

"What about?"

"Remember that rat that got run over? The one I buried in the yard?"

I nod.

"He was alive! He ran up my arm and tickled me with his whiskers."

"Yuck."

"No, it was nice. And people were patting him like he was a dog, like Bobo."

I don't say anything.

"And you know what else? Jess was there, and she was singing."

"Jerry! I forgot to tell you— I might know where she is!" I repeat what the clerk at Dollar Discount said. "Doesn't that sound like Mr. Molloy?"

His crooked grin lights up his face.

= = = = = = = = = = = = = = =

"You know I could be wrong."

I try to sound matter-of-fact. Jerry and Bobo and I are standing outside Mr. Molloy's door that afternoon. His car isn't out front, so he may be at work or shopping for groceries. I'm about to ring his bell anyway when Jerry points. "Charlie, look!"

Jess *is* here. We stare into the sunporch. I look twice to make sure it's really her. Her feathers have grown back, and her color's better. Her cage is clean and bright, with a cloth draped over one end to give some shade. There's a little bowl of water in the bottom and some cut-up greens that look like spinach next to that. She flies from perch to perch, showing off, as if she knows we're here.

We come closer, leading Bobo, to get a better view. The casement windows are wide open. "Sing, Jess!" Jerry whistles a couple of notes. She turns and looks at him. Her black eyes shine. You can tell that she remembers.

He whistles again. I see her throat begin to swell. Through the open window, her song trills and rises. I close my eyes and let myself go free.

= = = = = = = = = = = = = = =

"Charlie." Jerry tugs at my shorts.

"What?"

"There's someone."

At the back of the sunporch is a woman. She's short and small, with dark hair and Asian eyes. She's wearing a simple light green dress with gold embroidery around the neck and sleeves. When she sees us looking at her, she turns and hurries away.

"Who's that?"

"I don't know, but we should leave before she calls the police."

"I'm *not* leaving. We haven't done anything wrong. And I haven't seen Jess for weeks."

Now the front door opens, and Mr. Molloy steps out, smiling.

= = = = = = = = = = = = = = =

"I've wanted to call you ever since I picked him up, but I couldn't remember your last name."

"Jess is a girl."

"Actually, she's a he, but Jess fits boys and girls, so it doesn't really matter." He opens the door. "Come inside, so you can see him."

"We've got our dog."

"I noticed. But he can come in, too."

"His name is Bobo," Jerry explains.

"Bobo—an elegant name, if I do say so." He ushers us inside his house.

It's different from any place I've ever been. Dark red rugs cover the floors and hang from some of the walls. The couch is brown suede, and the wooden chairs are carved, like statues. There's a fireplace made of stone, with paintings over the mantel. Bookcases are everywhere.

He's leading us to the sunporch when the woman appears again. He puts his arm around her. "This is my wife, Tuyen."

I feel shy because she's different, but Jerry doesn't notice. "You have our canary. She's called Jess."

Mr. Molloy says that in another language. She giggles. When she smiles, her face is beautiful.

= = = = = = = = = = = = = =

We sit with them and Jess in their backyard. Beside our table, water pours from a swan's mouth into a mosaic pool filled with goldfish. A vine along the tall wood fence is heavy with purple flowers. You can smell the honey smell from where we sit. Mr. Molloy's chair is lined with gold and blue cushions. It's extra big so he'll be comfortable.

Tuyen brings tea on a bamboo tray, with tiny cups for all

of us. The tea is sweet and tastes like fruit. She can only speak a little English.

"You . . . likes birds?

"You . . . likes yellow bird?

"What are you names?"

Mr. Molloy doesn't correct her. He watches her like we watch Jess—as if just seeing her takes him someplace far-away and wonderful.

= = = = = = = = = = = = = =

Later he tells us what he did to make Jess well.

"Fresh greens, vitamins, a bowl of water to bathe in, and some room to exercise, that's what he needed. And TLC. He loves attention."

"Are you going to keep her?"

"Unless you think you have a prior claim."

"My mom said no," Jerry tells him glumly. "We tried and tried, but she won't change her mind."

"You do have Bobo."

Jerry kisses Bobo's head.

= = = = = = = = = = = = = =

They invite us back, not just "anytime," but Tuesday at six o'clock. Tuyen will cook food from Vietnam, which is where she's from. Jerry explains he's vegetarian. That doesn't seem to bother her. I think suddenly of Shan. She'd love to see their house. But I'm embarrassed to ask if she can come.

Walking down the front steps of their place is like stepping out of heaven into the cold, cold world. I wait until they close their door to reach for Jerry's hand.

Twenty-seven

It's Saturday, so I call Shan at home. The minute I hear her voice, I know that something's wrong.

"What's up?" she asks briskly.

"Want to hang out at McDonald's?"

"I can't. I have too much to do."

"Like what?"

"Like . . . stuff."

"But what about the videos we wanted to get? You know, for tonight?"

"Oh." Her voice softens. "Maybe. I'll have to ask."

"Is something wrong?"

"No, I'm just busy." She sounds phony. Her mom and dad must be nearby. I think she's about to hang up.

I blurt out, "We found Jess."

"Charlie, that's wonderful! Did Mr. Molloy have her?"

"Him and his wife. She's from Vietnam. And she gave us special tea, and they invited Jerry and me to dinner on Tuesday. Shan, you should see their house—it's so beautiful. They even have a fountain and a goldfish pond in their backyard."

"Ohhhhh." She sounds like her old self. "I want to come—not Tuesday, but the next time."

"Why not Tuesday?"

"'Cause I wasn't invited, dummy."

"Oh." I feel stupid.

"But tell them you have a friend—your very best friend—and that she'd love to meet them, too."

"I will."

Still, when I hang up the phone, something doesn't feel quite right.

Without Shan, I'm bored. So I end up spending part of the morning doing grocery shopping with Mom. I haven't gone with her for years, and when I tell her I'm interested, she looks shocked. Then she smiles. "I'd love to have you come."

= = = = = = = = = = = = = =

Mom drives an old Astro van with a "good luck doll" from Central America dangling from the mirror. She claims if you rub it, good things happen. On the passenger seat she has a bottle of water and a stack of tapes, a hairbrush, makeup, and a sweater. It's cozy here, like a little house on wheels. Mom glances at me sideways. "Is there something you want from the store, Charlie?"

"Not really."

"I've been thinking—now that you're getting older—that you might like to pick out some lipstick or some nail polish. I can show you how to put them on."

It's not that I haven't been thinking about that, because I have. But the truth is that, right now, all I want is her. Of course I don't tell her that, because she'd ask why. So I smile and rub the good luck doll. I want to tell her about Junie's leaving, but I can't, so instead I say, "Other kids get to go places—like Chicago. I've never been anywhere."

Mom smiles and pats my leg. "You've been to Pennsylvania, to Aunt Ellen's."

"Fawn Grove is right across the border. I might as well be here."

"I'm sure you'll get to travel. Last year Western took a graduation trip to New York City. And if you decide to go to college, you'll have lots of choices."

Mom turns right, into the Safeway parking lot. She looks in the rearview mirror, fluffs her hair, pulls the ends out between her fingers. "That's better." Then she adds, "I've got a list. With you here, too, we'll be done in half an hour."

= = = = = = = = = = = = = =

I came to the Safeway every Saturday till I turned ten. Back then I mostly begged for candy or cheap toys or money for the gum machine. This time is different. Mom gives me half her list: produce, bread, milk. "Pick out what looks good to you. Just make sure you get enough to last us through the week."

I push my cart to the produce aisle. Let's see—bananas for Jerry's cereal and Mom's lunch. . . . The peaches smell great, so I fill up a bag. Then I remember how Mom checks them for bruises, so I take them out and turn each one over in my hand. They're soft and beautiful. I get a head of broccoli and a cabbage so we can have coleslaw, two bags of salad greens, and a jar of blue cheese dressing, which I love. Then a couple of tomatoes—I check those over, too. Last but not least, a container of baby carrots. Then on to the dairy case for cheese slices and yogurt. I stand in front of it, facing the labels. *Week after week*, I tell myself. *Week after week, we've done this, all my life, and nothing bad has happened.* But from somewhere far away, Mr. Healy's soft voice answers, like he knows exactly what I'm thinking. *"Watch out."*

= = = = = = = = = = = = = =

I call Shan back when we get home, to see about the videos. Like before, she tries to brush me off. This time I march straight across the street to her front door. The curtains in the living-room windows are drawn, but I see movements through the cloth. I knock and ring the bell. Someone flips a bolt lock on the door and opens it.

Mrs. Johnson smiles when she sees me, but her face is taut. She hesitates. I hear Shan's dad: "Who is it?"

"Charlie."

He comes to the door, too. "Shan can't go out right now."

I wait for them to ask me in, but they don't. Then I hear Shan.

"Who's there?"

"Charlie."

She comes and stands behind them. "Come on in."

"No, Shan." Mr. Johnson shakes his head.

"Dad, this is Charlie! She's practically my sister!"

There's a moment of silence. I feel like disappearing. Then slowly, quietly, the front door closes in my face.

Twenty-eight

I go to the boulevard to get some videos to watch by myself. I pass McDonald's, Exxon, and the Laundromat. Just as I'm pulling open the door to Blockbuster, I hear somebody say my name. A hand grips my arm, too tight. I think of Jim, but before I can turn my head, someone else's voice hisses in my ear.

"Don't say a word," Junie says.

= = = = = = = = = = = = = =

He leads me into the back corner of Dollar Discount. Among boxes of laundry detergent and bleach, he looks me in the eye. "We're leaving," he says. "That's why they wouldn't let you in."

"You're going to Chicago. Shan told me, but I'm not supposed to know."

"Nobody's supposed to know—not just for my sake, either."

"Then how come you're telling me?"

"To warn you. You and Jerry were seen talking to the raincoat man. When he gives his papers to the police, everyone who knows him could be blamed for what goes down."

I shrug, but I'm only pretending I'm not scared. "Who knows what's in those papers? Crazy as Jim is, it may be gibberish."

"It's not."

I look up at him, surprised. "You mean you've read them?"

"Yes. He showed me, because he thought that I knew something, too."

"You said you sent him packing."

He nods. "I was afraid. Then he came back and told me there were others who had told the truth. He said he only needed one more statement." Junie sighs, a long sigh that seems to push the world outside us far away. "So I told him what I knew."

"You know who did it!" I start going haywire. Junie shoves his hand over my mouth to keep me quiet. I bite down, tasting the salt of his skin, but he doesn't flinch. He keeps holding on to me. I'm trembling. A tall man in a red hat, dragging a little kid, comes looking for some soap. He sees us, backs up, and turns the other way.

"Settle down," Junie says. "You need to know what's going on."

"He's going to tell the manager you're hurting me."

"No, I saw his hat move toward the door. People are scared. They don't want to get involved."

He looks around. There's a hallway with a water fountain leading to the bathroom. We step in there.

"Mr. Healy saw some deals go down. He called the police, and they busted two runners and scored a lot of crack. Later, the dealers found out who had turned them in."

"Why weren't they put in jail?"

"They were, but a few days later, they were out on bail. They decided to kill Mr. Healy so he couldn't be a witness at the trial. And as a warning. After he died, who would dare to testify against them?"

"Who did it?"

"They sent Kyle. He persuaded Jay to go with him. But Kyle couldn't do it, so one of the leaders, Juan, went back with the two of them."

I feel like I'm going to throw up. Junie must see that. His arms steady me. "Don't pass out," he says roughly.

I don't know how long we stand there, me slumping and him holding me up. He tells me Kyle came crying afterward and told him the whole story. I don't want to hear about Kyle feeling bad. There's a knot of hatred in my chest—for Junie, too, because he knew and didn't tell. Maybe I say so, because he shrugs and his voice is hard. "How you feel about me doesn't matter now. What matters is, until they're arrested—even after they're arrested—you and Jerry know nothing. Stay off the corner and out of the alleys until the whole thing is over."

"But if they're in jail—"

"They have others who will back them up. And they'll do whatever they can to stifle witnesses. The only hope is numbers. If there are enough people to testify, and others to support the ones who do, then we might win. The gangs can take out one or two of us, but they can't kill a whole neighborhood."

"When is all this going to happen?"

"Jim's giving the papers to the police on Monday. He's going into the hospital the same day. That way he won't be killed for what he's done."

"What about the ones who gave him evidence?"

He looks down at me.

"*That's* why you're going to Chicago."

He nods.

"What about the others?"

"I don't know who they are. Jim left the names off the evidence he showed me for their own protection."

"The police will know."

"And hopefully keep quiet. Otherwise, the case will never go to trial."

"Will you come back to testify?"

He nods.

"But what about Shan and your mom and dad? After you leave, couldn't the dealers take it out on them?"

"You didn't listen to what I said."

"What?"

"We're leaving. Not just me, Charlie. They're coming to Chicago, too."

= = = = = = = = = = = = = =

Junie's flying out Tuesday morning with his mom. He claims that she'll be checking job transfers and real estate. Shan and their dad will stay at home and do what's needed to prepare their house for sale. Everything's a big, huge secret. I don't believe it—why should I? All this time Junie has been lying about what he knew.

Twenty-nine

On Sunday, Mom, Jerry, and I go to Mass. Dad stays home because he wants to cut the lawn and watch the Orioles pregame show. I say a prayer for my family and one for Shan, like I usually do. I ask God to keep her safe and let her live on Lanvale Street across from me, no matter where Junie goes.

After church, we walk to Baskin-Robbins for ice cream. Jerry drags Mom into the Exxon to see the cats. He tells her all their names and cracks the car door so she can meet Baldy. Afterward, he quizzes her to see how many she remembers. She rolls her eyes at me when he's not looking, then puts her finger to her lips so she and I don't start laughing. Jerry doesn't even notice.

I don't see Shan till Monday at the Laundromat. When I come in, she's plopped down at the table staring at a tangle of sheets and towels. "I didn't know anything, Charlie. Junie told me the same day he told you."

"Kyle and Jay. . . . Can you believe it, Shan?"

"Not really. I mean, Kyle and Junie were like this." She puts two fingers close.

"And Kyle sat on Mr. Healy's porch and ate ice cream and listened to stories, just like us."

"He had problems reading . . ."

"That's no excuse! He could have gone to Ms. Essie! She would have done anything to help him!"

Shan nods, but she sounds sad instead of angry. "Junie said Kyle cried afterward, and asked for help. Junie didn't know what to do. He was sick to his stomach and going crazy, knowing what had happened. But he knew that if he told, he'd be in danger, too."

"So he's going away." I push his voice out of my mind: *"Not just me, Charlie. . . ."*

"Mom and Dad are totally flipped out. They think a witness in a murder trial involving drugs is like a sitting duck. They want Junie gone before the gangs realize where the evidence is from."

"Won't the police want to question him?"

"They set up an interview at the station today. I guess Jim turned in the papers early this morning."

"So he was right about Judgment Day."

"Telling who did it isn't justice. The jury will have to believe the witnesses enough that they'll vote guilty. Jim can't testify if he's in a mental hospital. And if Junie doesn't come back for the trial, there may not be a case."

"He's going to come back."

"That's what *he* says. But Mom and Dad don't want him to. I get the feeling they wish Junie hadn't told Jim anything."

"Then Kyle would have gotten away with what he did."

"I know. But there wouldn't be this talk about Chicago. . . ."

"What about Chicago?"

Shan stares at me. I guess she knows that I'm pretending.

"Don't worry," she says. "I'm not moving anywhere, no matter what they say."

= = = = = = = = = = = = = =

The laundry work is done. I get up, thinking we'll go to McDonald's. But Shan says no.

"My dad won't let me. He wants me to take a taxi home."

"A taxi! It's only three blocks!"

She rolls her eyes. "I know. But you can come with me, if you want."

I don't tell Shan, but this is the first time I've ridden in a taxi. And it's just about the dumbest thing I've ever done.

For three blocks, it costs four dollars! The driver thinks we're nuts. Shan says, "My dad asked if you'd wait here until I get into the house." He snorts, then sits there smoking a cigarette until we go inside and lock the door.

The house is all messed up. For a minute I think someone got in, but Shan shakes her head. "Dad's been going through things, sorting out what we really need and packing the rest in cardboard boxes."

"Do you really think you can convince him not to move?"

"He's upset now. After they arrest those boys, he'll calm down and reconsider. Believe me, Charlie, I've got this under control."

= = = = = = = = = = = = = =

We look through Shan's things. I know her room by heart: the posters and camp certificates on the walls, photographs of friends and cousins stuck around the curved oak frame of her mirror. In her closet, she's got clothes from years ago.

"Why in the world do you keep this?" I hold up a blue dress with smocking on the front, size eight.

"I wore that to your birthday party—don't you recall? That was the year I gave you the giant bubble wand."

I smile and pretend to remember. Shan has always cared more about clothes than I have.

"This is the coloring book Freddy Martin gave me for Christmas before his family moved to Boston."

"He was nice."

"This is the first lipstick I ever bought."

"It's empty, Shan."

"I know, but I want it anyway."

"What did you save from when you first met Ray?"

"You know me better than anyone." She shows me a napkin from McDonald's. Ray's name and phone number are printed across the top. "He called me, Charlie—last night. But I couldn't really talk to him. My folks were so worried that I'd mention something about Junie. . . ."

"Did you ever tell him about being an atheist?"

She's looking through her jewelry box. "Yes."

"How did it go?"

"Not very well. At first he didn't believe me. He thought I hadn't been to the right church, and if I tried his, I'd feel different. But I explained that I'd been an atheist for a long time, that it made sense to me, and I wasn't going to change my mind. Then he argued: 'How do you explain our being here on Earth?' I described the idea of evolution and said, 'I think that *we* choose what we're meant to do.' After that he got real quiet."

"He didn't break up with you."

"No. But I don't think he can accept me as I am."

"You haven't given him a chance! That was only one conversation!"

"I know. And he's going to call again tonight. . . ."

When she looks up, she's holding something in her hand. "Remember this bracelet, Charlie? I got it from my grandmother when I was ten. I never really liked it, but you did."

It's silver, with polished gems arranged around the narrow band.

"Why don't you take it? I don't think I'll wear it. Here."

"You shouldn't give me this. It's probably valuable."

"Take it. You'll enjoy it, and I won't."

I hold it in my hand. The stones are green and blue, jade and turquoise.

"I want to give you something, too."

"What?"

"I don't know. . . ." All I'm wearing is an orange lanyard that I made at day camp years ago and a ring with blue glass in the center. I don't even know where it came from.

"Take your pick."

She goes from one to the other, peering at them as if she's making the most important decision of her life. "The ring," she says finally. I take it off, and she slips it on her pinkie. "Now we're married." She giggles, but somewhere, under her words, there's sadness.

Thirty

Jerry doesn't know who killed Mr. Healy or about Junie's trip to Chicago. He and Bobo and I are walking home from day care that same afternoon. He's in a whiny mood, dragging his sneakers on the cracked concrete.

"Hurry up, Jerr. You're taking forever, and you're wearing out your shoes."

He's inching along. It's like he's moving in slow motion. "I don't want to."

"How come?"

"I want to go to Uncle Mac's instead."

"You should have asked me this morning. Now I've made other plans."

"What other plans?"

"To hang around with Shan."

"You're with her all the time. It's like I don't exist."

"Don't be ridiculous. I take care of you every single day."

"No, you don't." He stops and squints at me through his glasses. Then he mumbles something I can't hear.

"What?"

"Stop bugging me!" He crouches down to see some ants. "I'll be there in a minute."

Bobo and I walk farther down the alley. I told Shan that I'd be home by four o'clock. When I look back over my shoulder, Jerry's gone.

= = = = = = = = = = = = = = =

I'm furious, at him and me! I should have guessed that he was up to something. I run back the way we came. "Jerry, Jerry!" Dogs bark, and Bobo snarls and bares his teeth. There's no sign of him. "Damn!"

I reach the boulevard. The usual gang are hanging on the corner. Mr. Tibby looks bad today; his eyes are rimmed in red, and his pupils flick back and forth as if they're playing tag. One of his shoes is split along the side, so it looks like his foot's misshapen. But he smiles when he sees me. "You looking for Jerry? He crossed here a minute ago, running like his pants was on fire. He didn't even wait for the light to change."

Now the street is filled with traffic. I have to wait. The light takes forever. When it turns green, I take off, pulling Bobo behind me.

It takes three minutes to get to the Exxon. By then I'm

gasping for breath. Uncle Mac is under a Honda Civic. "Have you seen Jerry?" I holler down.

"I haven't seen anybody."

"Did he come in?"

"Not that I know of. You can check the office, if you want." The cats are terrified of Bobo. They hiss and leap in every direction. I'm in the middle of swirling fur. Bobo starts barking. "Jerry, are you here?"

No answer.

＝ ＝ ＝ ＝ ＝ ＝ ＝ ＝ ＝ ＝ ＝ ＝ ＝ ＝ ＝

I don't know what pulls me to the alley behind the boulevard, but as I turn that way, a feeling of weightlessness comes over me. It's as if my sneakers aren't even slapping against the pavement. "Jerry!" The space is lined with Dumpsters from the stores that face the front. Farther down, black plastic bags are piled high, waiting to be picked up. They stink like garbage. I pass behind Dunkin' Donuts, the Laundromat. Then my heart starts banging against my ribs like a prisoner rattling the bars of his cell. Jay-Jay, Kyle, and another man are leaning against the wall behind the Dollar Discount. Jay-Jay's facing my way, but the others have their backs to me. The stranger's tall and slim. And walking right down the middle of the alley, only about five feet away from them, is Jerry.

I'm not sure what to do. I know how dangerous they are, but Jerry doesn't. Maybe he'll walk on by; or maybe, if he speaks to them, they'll just ignore him. I slink along the wall with Bobo, hide behind a Dumpster.

They don't notice Jerry until he passes them and turns around. Even then they pay no attention. They're talking about music. One of the voices is Kyle's, but the stranger's is also familiar. I can't remember where I heard it. Maybe it was at the morgue that day when I saw Jim.

"He sold a million just that cut. He don't need more contracts."

"Man, they can't quit. Agents won't let 'em."

"Where'd you hear that?"

"Everybody knows. . . ."

Jay-Jay notices Jerry. "You lost, bro?"

He shakes his head.

"Go on, then."

Jerry shakes his head again. The others turn around. I stop breathing. Kyle speaks. "Why are you back here, Jerry? Did you and Uncle Mac lose a cat?"

"He ain't your uncle, man," Jay cracks. Jerry shakes his head.

They keep looking at him. Kyle says, "Go on."

"I won't."

"You want something?"

Jerry nods.

"What?"

His voice quavers. "I want you to repent."

They glance at each other. "What are you talking about?"

"Mr. Healy." The words are so soft I hardly hear them.

"Who's he?" The stranger seems baffled, but Jay-Jay and Kyle look suddenly alert.

"He was my neighbor on Lanvale Street. Somebody shot him."

Now there's an explosion of voices so intense and jumbled I can't make out the words.

Jerry doesn't speak until they're done. "Jim sent me here to talk to you," he says.

"Who's Jim?"

"The raincoat man. He said to tell you there are witnesses."

"Witnesses to what?" Jay-Jay looks confused, maybe even a little scared. But Kyle moves closer. "What witnesses?"

I'm clutching the edge of the Dumpster like it's going to run away.

"I don't know who, but Jim gave evidence to the police. He said to tell you that you will be judged. If you confess, it's not too late to save your soul."

Jay's eyes open wide. He takes a step backward.

The stranger's voice is like a whip. "Didn't we tell you to disappear?"

"You still have time," Jerry says.

Jay's leaning up against the back of the discount store. "I told you all I didn't want nothing to do with—"

"Shut up!" The tall man spins like a dancer and slaps Jay-Jay in the face.

"Juan, why'd you—"

"Shut up!" He turns back, reaches for Jerry's face, snatches his glasses off, and hurls them down the alley. He grabs him by his skinny shoulders. "You little fool. . . ."

Jerry starts crying. Bobo can tell that he's in trouble. He lunges forward, and I'm yanked from behind the Dumpster. For a minute they don't see me. But Bobo breaks free, rushes to Jerry, and licks his face. Juan backs up. Kyle stares at me like I'm a ghost. "Charlie. . . ." His eyes go blank. "What are you doing here?"

"Jerry ran away, and I came after him."

"You shouldn't be back here." Kyle's voice is soft. Maybe he remembers how we played SPUD behind the school on Sunday afternoons.

Jay-Jay's sniffling. "I didn't want nothing—"

"Shut *up,* man!" Kyle turns into another person right in front of me. He jumps forward and hits Jay, and he falls down. When Jay-Jay gets back up, he's crying. He keeps his hand over his mouth.

The man called Juan glares at us as if we're roaches that just crawled out from behind the woodwork. His gaze radiates anger so deep and strong that I feel like I'm dissolving in front of him. He flips his jacket open. I see the handle of a pistol tucked inside his pants.

"We know where you live," he whispers.

Bobo growls.

The three of them turn their backs on us. Jay is limping as they walk away.

= = = = = = = = = = = = = =

Jerry's on his knees, searching for his glasses. After a few minutes, he finds them near a pile of broken glass and puts them on. "They're scratched. . . . Look, Charlie, they have a scratch on them."

My teeth are clacking against each other.

"I can't see right!" He starts crying. I pat his back awhile. He begins to hiccup, then calms down. "You brought Bobo."

"No kidding." Jerry doesn't understand what just went down. If they'd wanted to, they could have killed us both.

"I did what Jim said," Jerry murmurs. "He left me a signal—a white sock on Mr. Healy's hedge. That's how I knew it was today."

"What he asked of you was really dangerous."

"He said they wouldn't hurt a little kid."

"They'll hurt anyone who's in their way."

"Not Kyle."

"Jerry, don't you understand what they were saying?"

He looks up at me through the filthy lenses of his glasses. There's a little wrinkle line in his forehead that he gets when he's thinking. For a while his eyes are blank. Then something flashes, and he gets it. "It was them. . . ."

"Of course it was them! Why else did you ask them to repent?"

"Because Jim said to." He looks down the alley. There's garbage and broken glass all over. You can smell stale beer from the trash cans behind the bar. Jerry is so pale he's almost gray.

He grabs my hand and whispers, "I want Jess."

= = = = = = = = = = = = = =

We look at her through the Molloys' sunporch window. When she sees us, she flaps her wings and hops around her cage. Jerry whistles a little tune. Her throat swells, and she begins to sing.

Thirty-one

We're sitting on my front porch. I didn't tell Shan what happened in the alley yesterday—she has enough to worry about right now. Junie and his mom left for Chicago this morning. Shan skipped work and went with them to the airport. She had to stop at the security station by the gates, so she couldn't watch them getting on the plane. "You won't believe this, but I bawled my eyes out," she tells me. "You would have thought I would never see them again."

= = = = = = = = = = = = = = =

Marcus comes riding past on his bike. When he sees us, he spins around, jolts across the grass, and slams on the brakes. His face, usually round and smiling, looks like a balloon that's been leaking all night long.

"You heard what happened, right?" His voice is low.

"What?"

"The cops came to our house after supper. They were shouting and banging on the door. When Aunt Lily opened it, they pushed past her with their guns drawn. Kyle was in the bathroom, but they wouldn't even wait till he came out. They kicked the door open and handcuffed him while he was in his underwear."

Shan and I don't move. "What did they want him for?" I manage to squeak out.

"I don't know, because Aunt Lily made me go outside. I could hear them yelling at each other. Then they put Kyle in the squad car and drove away."

"You don't know why?"

He shakes his head. I can tell he's real upset.

"Were you scared?"

"Yeah, 'specially when I saw the guns."

"I would have been, too," Shan says.

I get him ice cream and cookies, because I feel bad for him. Marcus doesn't have anything to do with Kyle's problems. He probably never hurt a bug in his whole life.

"He should get out tomorrow," Marcus says, when he's done eating. Shan and I look at each other and keep quiet.

= = = = = = = = = = = = = =

Mom drives Jerry and me to the Molloys'. She says hello at the front door and thanks them for inviting us over. That makes me feel like a baby. I wonder if I'll find anything to talk about. But it turns out to be easy: There are birds and food and places in the neighborhood. Tuyen has never even been to McDonald's. Jerry and I promise to take her. Mr. Molloy rolls his eyes, because he doesn't care for McDonald's food. He's afraid if Tuyen likes it, she'll stop cooking and ask for Big Macs every night.

I can see why he's worried. She makes things we've never tasted: curries and spring rolls and a noodle dish with sprouts and peanuts on top. The food's not boring, even though it's vegetarian. We eat it on their backyard patio, beside the goldfish pond. Jerry says we're going to make a pond, too. I look at him hard: "Since when?" He shrugs and says we are, he just hadn't told anyone about it yet.

Back in the house, we take Jess out of her cage and let her fly around. She lights on Tuyen's shoulder, flapping her wings. Tuyen speaks to her in Vietnamese, and Mr. Molloy adds something else in French. Each of them can speak four languages. "Four!" Jerry can't believe it. "I can hardly talk one."

Before we leave, Tuyen volunteers to teach us how to cook spring rolls this coming Saturday. We both say yes, and I tell her about Shan, and she invites her, too. We think that we'll walk home, but Mr. M. says no. Jerry loves the car. He asks questions about the engine and the brakes. There are men and boys gathered on the corner, but Mr. M.

doesn't seem to notice them. I scrunch down in the seat. *"We know where you live. . . ."* When we get home, he waits until we get inside the house before he drives away.

= = = = = = = = = = = = = =

I'm at the Laundromat the next morning. Shan's worried about her dad. "I thought he'd feel better once Junie left, but instead he's focusing on me. He dropped me off this morning, and I'm supposed to go straight home the minute I'm finished work. If he knew I was going to McDonald's, he'd kill me."

"We could go to your house. Yesterday was nice."

"All that mess. . . ." Shan shakes her head, remembering her room, I guess. "Anyway, Ray's coming."

"Have you told him what's going on?"

"No, I just said there's a family problem, and I can't explain till it's over. He knows something's strange, because he called again last night, but I could hardly talk to him. Dad's afraid I'll slip and say something I'm not supposed to, so he rushes me off the phone." Shan sighs. "You come, too, Charlie. Okay?"

= = = = = = = = = = = = = =

McDonald's is the usual soap opera. Today Megan is thinking she'll break up with Joe. He never has any money, and yesterday she saw him talking to another girl. Ray chuckles.

"Come back next week for the next installment." He reaches across the table and takes Shan's hand. She looks embarrassed, but I can tell she's happy. He smiles at me, too, so I won't feel left out. We talk about small stuff: TV shows and music. He's so nice, I'm jealous. Ray asks questions about my family. His uncle used to work at the GM plant where Dad is now. "He got worried that they'd move to Mexico, so he went back to school and learned computer programming," he says.

"My dad's worried about that, too." Ray has a little sister the same age as Jerry. Shan just sits there smiling while we get to know each other.

After a while I leave, so the two of them can be alone. I don't know if Shan takes a taxi home or not.

= = = = = = = = = = = = = =

Jerry and I are playing Monopoly on the front porch when Marcus comes by on his bike. He steps off and lets the bike fall forward on the grass.

"Want to play Monopoly?"

"No, thanks."

Jerry's trotting the little metal dog around the board. He lands on Pacific Avenue. I have three houses and a hotel on it, so he's bankrupt. He throws his money at me. "I quit."

"Sore loser."

"No, I'm not. I want to start the goldfish pond."

"What goldfish pond?"

"The one I told you about last night."

He walks around the backyard. It's so full of grave markers that it's hard for him to find a place to put the pond. Finally he settles on a sunny spot beside the rose-bush. But he's too weak and skinny to dig the hole; when he stands on the back of the shovel blade, it hardly sinks in. I take it away and stand on it myself. The blade slices down a few inches. We scoop out a hunk of dirt. Marcus takes the shovel then. He's strong. In a few minutes we've got a hole two feet across. Bobo jumps into the hole and digs, too, spraying dirt on all of us. We're so sweaty that it sticks. We go into the kitchen and wipe it off with paper towels. Then we decide we need iced tea and cookies. While I'm getting the ice, Jerry looks out the window at what we've done.

"Hey," he says suddenly, "there's someone in the alley."

"Who?"

"I don't know. I never saw him before."

Marcus looks out, too. "Me, neither."

By the time I get there, the man is gone. He was proba-bly on his way someplace and took the shortcut, like Jerry and I do.

"We know where you live. . . ."

"Shut up!" I tell myself, but the voice has latched on to a

spot inside my head, and no matter how hard I try to shake it off, it won't let go.

= = = = = = = = = = = = = =

Mom and Dad don't scoff at Jerry's plan. In fact, they're into it, so tonight we're all in the backyard again. Dad says that when the hole is done, we'll have to buy a plastic liner, like a baby's swimming pool. And a pump to move the water: "Otherwise, it will get stagnant." We'll get goldfish and water lilies from the aquarium store. "The plants return oxygen to the water so the fish can breathe," he explains. I wonder how he knows all this.

Mom's thinking about the fountain. She says there're lots of designs to choose from—swans and frogs and turtles and fish that shoot water from their mouths. She's excited. "After dark, we'll bring our chairs out by the pool and look up at the stars," she says.

= = = = = = = = = = = = = =

Jerry's so wound up that he can't sleep. He keeps running into my room with drawings of the goldfish pond. Finally I get sick of it. "If you come in here one more time, I'm telling Mom and Dad."

His feelings are hurt. "The pond was my idea. If you're not nice to me, you can't participate."

"*Participate*—where'd you learn that?"

"From Mrs. Brill."

"Well, if you don't *participate* in turning off your light and going to bed, I'm going to kick your skinny little butt."

"Not!" Jerry flounces out. I let myself drift off to sleep. The traffic from the corner by the boulevard makes a soft *whoosh whoosh*, like the shushing of a baby. Then comes the sound of wind and, on it, voices: *"We know where you live. . . ."*

Thirty-two

Jay confesses to the police. Shan says he's turned state's evidence; he'll testify against the others at the trial to get a lighter sentence. "The police are going to keep him in a separate wing of the prison so that he'll be safe."

"So Junie won't have to be a witness?"

"No, they still need him. Otherwise, the defense can claim Jay made up his story to get off easy." We're sitting on her bed, taking a break from sorting out her stuff. "Now that he's confessed, they'll all be stuck in jail until the trial."

"That's good." But I remember something Junie said: *"They have others who will back them up. . . . The only hope is numbers. . . . The gangs can take out one or two of us, but they can't kill a whole neighborhood."* I ask Shan, "Did he say that to your family, too?"

"Yes, and they agree. But they still want Junie gone.

That way there's no chance for the gangs to take revenge on him."

= = = = = = = = = = = = = =

Shan's room is even messier than before. "That's because I'm making piles," she explains.

"Which pile is this?"

"My toys—the ones I want to give my kids. Like this." She picks up one of the Barbies we used to play with. The doll's head wobbles on its narrow shoulders. "Remember, Charlie?"

"Of course I remember. We must have spent a million hours playing Barbie and Ken."

"No, I mean *this* Barbie."

"What about her?"

Shan grasps the body with one hand and the head with the other. She pulls. Barbie's head pops off. We both start laughing.

"Remember?" Shan asks. I nod. "That was the worst fight we ever had. This head reminds me that you can hate somebody's guts, but later you can change your mind."

= = = = = = = = = = = = = =

When I pick Jerry up, I tell him about Jay's confession. I tell him that in a strange way, the Day of Judgment was a true prophecy and that his talking to Jay-Jay in the alley was probably one reason he confessed. I say that the people who killed Mr. Healy will probably go to jail for their whole lives. He's happy, 'cause he thinks he helped Jay save his soul. "He won't have to go to hell. And maybe the others will repent, too, and save themselves. Jim said the time had come for good to spread around the world and conquer evil."

"That won't bring Mr. Healy back."

"He's in heaven, Charlie. Jim says he's watching us up there. He can hear us and see everything we do."

= = = = = = = = = = = = = =

Each morning at the Laundromat I hear the latest on Shan's dad.

"It's like those battery commercials. Someone picked him up and turned him in a certain direction, and now he can't turn back. Every day he sorts through more stuff to get rid of 'before we move.' I'm starting to think he wanted to go back to Chicago anyway, and the incident with Junie was the trigger that got him thinking it could really happen."

"Have you talked to your mom?"

"Yes. She called again last night. I told her I don't want to move, and she said that we'll all talk when she gets home next Monday. In the meantime, she thinks my room could use a going-over anyway."

"She might have a point."

Shan makes a face at me. She always says my room's too neat.

I can't wait for Shan to meet Tuyen. I describe her clothes: "I think they're silk, and in color combinations we don't wear: blues and greens together, oranges and yellows, too. The jackets have little stand-up collars, with gold or cream embroidery. Even the buttons are embroidered."

"I can't believe she's never come into the Laundromat. Maybe she's too shy."

I nod. "But not with Jerry. Her English isn't good, but she seems to understand him. She doesn't even think he's weird."

"Maybe she's too polite to say so. Or maybe she hasn't learned the word."

We start laughing. "Around here, she ought to learn it pretty quick."

= = = = = = = = = = = = = =

We go to McDonald's and sit in our usual booth. The french fries and Coke taste better than ever because Kyle, Juan, and Jay will be in jail for a long, long time. After a while Ray comes by. I guess he can tell we're feeling good. He buys us extra fries and shows us how he can whistle part of a Mozart symphony. He learned it from the stereo at the hospital. He has free tickets to the Orioles game this Sunday afternoon, and he asks us both to come. Shan says she'll have to ask her dad. I'm pretty sure that my folks will say yes, but I say I'll check, too, in case Shan can't. It wouldn't be fair for me to go with him alone.

= = = = = = = = = = = = = = =

We're sitting on the floor of Shannon's room. It's looking better. There are cartons stacked neatly along one wall, each one labeled with Magic Marker: *Shan, Halloween costumes; Shan, schoolwork, 4th and 5th grade; Shan, dolls.* Her bureau drawers can actually be closed because they aren't so stuffed with clothes. Although she complained while she was packing things away, now she's satisfied. "I still have everything, but now it's labeled so I can find it."

"Where will you put the boxes?"

"I'll keep them here."

"Against the wall?"

She nods happily.

"What do you think your mom will say?" Mrs. Johnson's known to be a neat freak, so she and Shan have had their differences.

"Nothing. She says she can't wait to see me. And I can't wait to see her, either. I guess the saying's true. *Absence makes the heart grow fonder.*"

"I've never been away from my mom, except when I've

spent the night at Aunt Ellen's. I'd love to go someplace on my own."

"Maybe if we both save up, we can go to Chicago next summer. . . ."

"Oh, wow!" Why hadn't I thought of that? "How much is the plane fare?"

"About two hundred dollars. . . ."

"We have plenty of time. . . ."

"But I need what I have right now for school clothes." Shan has her heart set on a Ralph Lauren sweater. She won't even tell *me* what it costs.

"Do you think Mr. Louras would hire us both?"

She makes a face. "Nice as he is, I'm counting down the days until I'm out of there."

"I thought you liked it."

"Are you kidding? Folding other people's underwear isn't exactly an out-of-body experience."

"Then how can we make money?"

"Baby-sitting, maybe, or walking dogs."

"You don't like dogs."

"I like Bobo."

"Maybe you could baby-sit, and I could walk the dogs. We could put an ad up in Dollar Discount: Baby- and pet-sitting service."

Shan's more excited than I've seen her in a while. "That's a great idea."

"I'll make the sign right now, while you're going through more stuff."

She gets me paper and Magic Markers. "Get to work."

= = = = = = = = = = = = = =

That night at dinner, I show the sign to Mom and Dad. For once they both approve of what we've done. Mom even says that she can use the copier at work to make more signs. When I bring up Chicago, they look at each other, but they don't say no!

After dinner, we work on the goldfish pond. Dad's brought sand to line the bottom of the hole so the plastic liner won't get torn. We figure out exactly where we'll put the fountain. We'll have to run an electric cord through the basement window. Mom plans some little flower beds to go around the goldfish pond. She wants Dad to build a patio with bricks and slate. If he does, we'll get new outdoor furniture.

"Where's all this money coming from?" Dad asks.

Mom doesn't back down: "Those green plastic chairs are only a few dollars each, and the tables aren't much more."

Dad shakes his head. "Next you'll be wanting a new house!" He tickles Jerry. "And it's all your fault!"

"How come?"

"Because you had the idea for the goldfish pond."

"I got that from the Molloys."

"So it's their fault. And they don't even know it!"

We all crack up then.

= = = = = = = = = = = = = =

When we come in, I call Shan to tell her about Chicago. But the line is busy, and later there's no answer.

Thirty-three

"**I**'ve got great news," I tell Shan the next morning.

She doesn't seem to hear me. "I talked to Mom again," she says. Her voice is flat, and when I get closer to the Formica table, I see her eyes are red.

"What's wrong?"

"She bought a house."

"What?"

"In Chicago."

"But I thought—"

"So did I. But they still think it's too dangerous to stay here. There was an incident a couple years ago where someone testified against a drug gang. A few months later, thugs waited till he left his house. Then they went inside and shot up everything that moved. His whole family was killed."

= = = = = = = = = = = = = =

The news that Shan is really moving takes a while to register inside my brain. Then, like a seed that's been waiting to flower, it blooms, and all I see is red. I feel childish, but I say it anyway: "You're going to Chicago! We were supposed to go next summer! I had it all worked out. Mom and Dad were going to let me do it. Mom's even making copies of our ad."

Shan's face flashes surprise. "You know I don't want to move."

"When you were little, Chicago was all you talked about—how great it was compared to here."

She shrugs. "I knew that Uncle James was there. Since he was my idol, the place he lived was special, too. We visited him, but I hardly remember anything—just a big lake and a zoo beside it. That could be anywhere."

"Except here. You'll never have to sit in this steaming Laundromat again."

"Don't say that, Charlie!" She gets even more upset. "This is my home."

"The Laundromat?" I'm being cruel, but I can't stop myself. The truth is, Shan will have a better life. "McDonald's? The Exxon? You certainly loved it there!"

"Everything I care about is here—"

"Not for long."

"Stop it!" Hurt darkens Shan's eyes, but I don't feel a thing.

= = = = = = = = = = = = = =

"There will be sacrifices," Jim had said.

= = = = = = = = = = = = = =

Once Shan's mom buys the house in Chicago, things happen fast. Mrs. Johnson delays her trip back home to set up bank accounts and find painters and carpenters for the new house. A Realtor comes to their house here and walks around inside, outside, up and down the block. She asks whether Mr. Healy's house is vacant. "It's been tied up in an estate settlement," Mr. Johnson explains. "It will go up for sale next month."

Shan and I make up again. She says she's talked to Ray and told him that she's moving. He's going to write her in Chicago. "It wouldn't have worked anyway," she says. "Our beliefs are so different." Shan's eyes fill up, but she shrugs it off and says, "At least Dad's letting me go to the ball game."

"I can't go—Mom needs my help in the backyard." I wonder if Shan knows I made that up. This way the two of them can be alone together in the little time they have left.

She has to quit the Laundromat to help her dad finish packing and cleaning up the house. On her last day there, we sit across from each other at the Formica table, folding T-shirts. She shows me a photograph of their new house. It reminds me of the row houses we have here, only it's called a town house, and it's covered with stucco instead of brick. "Mom says there are two delis and a coffee shop just down the block. She's seen teenagers in them talking and listening to music."

I don't like hearing about the place where Shan will sit across from some other girl instead of me.

Mr. Louras interrupts our talk. He takes away the T-shirts and then fishes a little package out of his suit pocket.

Shan's surprised. "You didn't have to buy me anything!" When she opens it, we see a tiny statue of a woman. She's graceful, even though one arm is partly gone.

"It's a copy of a relic from the ruins at Mycenae," he explains. "The world's greatest civilizations existed there."

Shan turns the figure over in her hands. "It's beautiful."

"To remember us by." He waves his hand around the room, meaning not just him but the Laundromat, I guess. To me, he says, "This job will be open, Charlene. And you have the experience."

"Thanks, but I have to take care of my little brother."

A smile flashes, then disappears. "Jerry's a nice boy, but socks can't run away from you."

After he leaves, I roll my eyes at Shan. "You can't keep a secret in this neighborhood, no matter how hard you try."

= = = = = = = = = = = = = =

Jerry wants to write to Jim. Of course, he doesn't mention this to Mom and Dad. Instead he shows me a letter he's already started:

> *Dear Jim,*
> *Do you like the hospitle?*
> *I did what you told me. Now 3 peopel are in jail,*
> *they cant come out.*

"I have to find out his address."

"Did he tell you what hospital he was going to?"

"Johns Hopkins. But he thought they'd send him back to a hospital in Texas."

"Oh." I remember the return address on that envelope so clearly that I could be looking at it now: *Marie Chalmers, 641 Reyes Street, Port Arthur, Texas.* But I don't say anything. Jim put Jerry in a lot of danger.

"Do you want to send a message in my letter?"

"I can write to him myself if I have anything to say."

= = = = = = = = = = = = = =

Marcus is convinced that Kyle is innocent. When we see him, he says the charges are phony.

"Kyle wouldn't have hurt Mr. Healy. He liked him, just like us."

"Maybe he was forced."

"By who?"

"Those gangs can own you, Marcus," Shan says gently. "They lure you in with money and drugs until, little by little, they steal your soul away. Then you're trapped and can't get out."

"Not Kyle. He didn't like them, 'cause they beat him up."

"But he went back."

"They said they'd hurt him even worse if he didn't."

Shan and I don't say anything.

"Anyway, he was sleeping in my room the night Mr. Healy was killed. If he'd left, I would have heard him." Marcus stares at his hands.

He knows and we know that he's lying. But Kyle is family. What else can Marcus do?

= = = = = = = = = = = = = =

On Saturday afternoon Shan, Jerry, and I are invited to Tuyen's to make spring rolls. Shan falls in love—with the furniture, the yard, Tuyen, and her lovely clothes. Even Jess seems wonderful to her. "In Dollar Discount, she was just a bird, but here she fits in with the colors and the atmosphere."

"She's a he," Mr. M. tells Shan.

"She is?" Shan looks at me.

"To me he'll always be a she, so I still call her that."

"Maybe I'll just call him *it*," Shan says. We *all* object to that. From then on, Shan just says "Jess."

To make the rolls, we chop carrots and Chinese cabbage and special radishes called daikon, then wrap the filling in squares of dough. Tuyen heats oil in a special pan she calls a wok. After all the rolls are made, she puts a few at a time into the hot oil and pokes them with a big flat spoon. When they've turned golden brown, she lifts them out and lets them dry on paper towels. We make twenty-three spring rolls. She piles them on a green tray and takes it to the patio. There's a special fruity sauce to dip them in. I try not to grab, but I see everybody's looking at what's left. Finally Mr. M. divides them into groups and deals them out: "One for you and you and you. . . ." He waits to see if anyone will say "I'm full," but no one does. We cut the last three rolls into pieces and gobble those down, too.

When we leave, Tuyen gives us each a hug—Shan, too. And Mr. M. drives us all home. He doesn't say anything when we pass the men on the corner, but he gets out of his car and waits until we're safe inside before he drives away.

= = = = = = = = = = = = = =

The next day I help Shan pack. Her dad says she has to cut the number of boxes she can take by half, from twenty-nine to fifteen. She's steaming mad. "Just because he doesn't care about his possessions doesn't mean I don't care about mine. Every one of these boxes is important to me."

I don't argue. I wouldn't want anybody telling me I had to get rid of my stuff, either.

By now Mr. Johnson has told the other families on the block about the move. He explains that schools are better in Chicago, and Karen, his wife, will have a higher-paying job. My folks are disturbed because, even though they aren't close friends with Shan's parents, they've been neighbors for a long time—twelve years of birthday parties, sleep-overs, borrowed videos, lending tools and sugar and spools of thread. Dad thinks they're making a mistake, but he doesn't tell them that. Of course, he doesn't know the truth about why they're leaving. I wonder what he'd do if Jerry or I had to testify.

Thirty-four

Mom's upset for me. She asks when I learned about the Johnsons' plan to move away.

"A few days ago. Her dad said to keep quiet, but Shan told me anyway."

"You two are like sisters." Mom shakes her head, like she doesn't feel good about what's happening. I swallow.

"Mom, Mr. Johnson's making Shan throw stuff away—important things. If she brought over some boxes, could we keep them for her?"

"We could fit a couple of cartons in the basement. Two or three, maybe."

"Good. I'll go tell her. She hates leaving anyway, 'cause all her friends are here. Losing things she cares about just makes it worse."

Mom stands at the sink, looking out the window into the

backyard. The blue liner's in the hole now. Next we'll pack stones and dirt around the edges of the pool. She sighs. "I think the Johnsons are worried about Junior. I'm sure you've heard that Kyle's in jail, and he and Junie had been friends. Leo and Karen may want Junie out of that circle of boys as fast as possible."

There's so much that Mom has no idea about. I choose my words carefully. "Junie wasn't selling drugs."

"I never said he was. But right or wrong, there's guilt by association. And it's hard to break away from old friends, even when they're heading down the wrong path."

"It's not fair to Shan, though. They should think about her, too."

"I feel sorry for her—and you—but Shan will survive the move. And she probably understands the situation. If Jerry was in trouble, wouldn't you do whatever we asked to help him out?"

"I—I guess."

"Of course you would, because he's your brother."

I stand beside her, looking out. Bobo's curled up, snoozing in the sun. Jerry's Popsicle crosses dot the right side of the yard. I wonder if they'll still be out there when he's nine or ten. Then I notice something moving in Mr. Healy's yard.

"Mom, did you see that?"

"It's just a person walking around."

"I never saw him before."

She smiles. "I know you've got this neighborhood under your wing, Charlie, but there might be one or two people you haven't met."

She can't hear the voice that whispers, *We know where you live. . . .*"

= = = = = = = = = = = = = = =

"You might as well see it now," Shan says. We're sitting on Mr. Healy's front steps. Yesterday Shan went to the Orioles game with Ray, and on the way back, on the number seven bus, he kissed her. She called me and told me the second she got home. I hadn't heard her sound so happy in a long, long time. But now—after we've gone over the date and the kiss in minute-by-minute detail—she has something else she wants to talk about. She hands me a folded sheet of paper. "Every house in this neighborhood will get one of these tomorrow."

COMMUNITY MEETING
On Saturday, August 25, at 12 noon
Corner Belair Boulevard and Lanvale Street
Subject: Drug sales in this neighborhood
For information, call 410–555–1212

I read it over twice, then look up slowly. "This is *your* phone number!"

Shan nods.

"Why are you doing this?"

"Dad and I talked. We decided that we don't want to slink out of the neighborhood like dogs with our tails between our legs. People need to know what's going on and that kids from around here are involved in it. If enough people come to the meeting—and he thinks they will— we'll all be safer, 'cause everyone will know what's happening. We won't be here to help with the solution, but at least we can speak out before we leave."

"But your dad's already worried about safety—"

"Kyle and Jay and Juan are in jail now, without bail. Junie's safe, and we'll be leaving Wednesday—"

"I'm afraid, anyway."

Shan puts her arm around my back. Suddenly I feel as limp as a wilted flower.

"Everything's changing . . ."

She rests her head on my shoulder. "One thing you can count on is we'll still be friends."

"Forever?"

"Sure. We got married, remember?" She's got that silly little ring I gave her on her pinkie. "See?"

≡ ≡ ≡ ≡ ≡ ≡ ≡ ≡ ≡ ≡ ≡ ≡ ≡ ≡

Mr. Johnson pays boys to distribute the flyers to everyone's front door. Marcus is chief of the troops. He's happy about the meeting, because now his aunt will have a chance to say that Kyle is innocent.

We help him with the flyers. Jerry and Bobo and I do Lanvale Street. It's back and forth on the sidewalks. We have lots of older people here, and many of them are home. "What's this?" they say, and then they read it over. Most of them look nervous. I have the feeling that more folks than I imagined knew what was going on. "Who else is coming to the meeting?" they ask. Nobody wants to be the only one there. I tell about Shan's dad. Everyone knows him, because her family's lived on our block so long. They ask about our folks.

"Mom and Dad aren't home yet, so they haven't seen the flyer."

They look uneasy as they close their doors.

Thirty-five

After we finish handing out the flyers, I take Jerry to Uncle Mac's. We haven't been there in a while, because we've gone to the Molloys' instead. But he's not thrilled to see us, anyway. There's something wrong with his hydraulic lift. He glares at it as if he'd like to kill someone. The cats must sense his mood, because they stay out of sight. Jerry and I sit on the workbench until he's finished what he's doing.

He pushes a button. The lift comes partway down, then makes a noise like it's being run into by a bus. Up—same noise. He bangs at something with a wrench, tries again. This time it isn't quite so loud. He bangs again, then throws the wrench down on the floor and turns around to us.

"Can we feed your cats?" Jerry asks.

"I guess." He's glum. "Come on in the back, and we'll see what's there."

= = = = = = = = = = = = = = =

He fills the aluminum pans with dry food, but he's out of milk today. The cats crowd around: Cisco, Angel, Brownie, Pretty Boy, China.

"I can feed Baldy," Jerry volunteers.

"No need. He jumped out of the car last week. I've been all around the neighborhood calling, but he hasn't come back."

"Baldy's gone!" Jerry starts bawling. "He was my favorite!" Awkwardly Uncle Mac leans down and pats him on the shoulder.

"That cat was a roamer from the word go. That's why he had so many scars. He's probably in the alley feasting on rats."

"But I miss him!"

"I do, too." Uncle Mac sighs. "Ever since I had him, it was Baldy's way or no way."

We ask if he knows Mr. M. Turns out Uncle Mac remembers people by their cars. "Molloy . . . Malibu 350?" he asks.

Jerry nods.

"Big guy, walks with a cane?"

"That's him. He and his wife bought the bird that used to be at Dollar Discount, the one Charlie and I liked. They're taking real good care of her. They have a couple of finches, too."

"He takes good care of that car. Changes the oil more than he needs to."

"His wife is from Vietnam."

"Is that right?"

But I can tell that Uncle Mac's still thinking about Baldy. Jerry and I promise we'll look for him, too.

= = = = = = = = = = = = = = =

We cross at the corner on our way home. Mr. Tibby's there. He nods, but his eyes look strange today, as if he's distracted or upset. There are a couple boys I don't know. Partway up the first block of Lanvale, I turn and look back. A white car pulls up right before the intersection; the window rolls down. A little face looks out the side. When she sees me, she cries out, smiling. It's Sara, of the white Saab. Before I can go back, one of the new boys tosses something through the open window. Sara's dad rolls it back up and speeds away.

= = = = = = = = = = = = = = =

Mom sees the flyer first, 'cause Jerry left it lying on the front step, even though it's our house and he could have brought it in. She reads it while she's kicking off her shoes. Then she flips it over, to see what's on the other side. She reads it again.

"Who brought this?" she asks.

"I did." Jerry's proud.

"Where did you get it?"

"Marcus was handing them out. Mr. Johnson's going to give him a nickel for each one that gets delivered. He asked me to help."

"From Leo. . . ." Mom nods, as if she's putting two and two together.

"Are you going?"

"Sure I am."

"What about Dad?"

"I can't speak for Dom." Sometimes he won't go to church or the PTA because he'd rather drink his beer and watch the football game. That makes Mom mad.

"Ms. Essie's going," Jerry says.

"Good. If you see her before Saturday, tell her I'll be right there at her side."

= = = = = = = = = = = = = =

Dad *doesn't* want to go to the meeting. He says there's evil in the world, and there always will be. "The cat tortures the mouse. You can't teach it not to," he explains. "But if you stand there watching the mouse suffer, you'll go crazy. You have to learn to put bad things out of your mind and go on living."

"You think that we can't make things better, but we can. We already have."

"Shhhh . . . ," I say. I don't want Jerry telling about the alley. But that's not what he has in mind.

"If Charlie hadn't told Mr. Molloy about Jess, she'd be dead now. But Charlie did tell him, and that caused him to save her life."

Dad's watching the news. "Who's Jess?"

Mom bops him on the head with her dishcloth. "That's the bird the kids were always talking about, at Dollar Discount."

"I didn't realize she was sick."

"Well, she was, and Charlie saved her life. Even Mr. M. said so."

"That's good." Dad looks up from the TV. "Good for you, Charlie."

"If she saved someone's life, then you can, too." Jerry's standing there with his arms folded. I used to be the only one who'd argue with Dad, but things have changed.

"Chill, Jerr." Dad tries to tickle him, but Jerry moves away.

Mom backs him up. "Dom, I think we need to hear what Leo has to say."

"Can't we just call him?"

All three of us stare at him so hard that he actually wriggles a little, as if our eyes make him uncomfortable. He sighs. "Okay, I'll come."

= = = = = = = = = = = = = =

Shan calls before I go to bed.

"Tomorrow we're driving around to say good-bye to

Mom and Daddy's friends. I won't be home till late, so I'll see you the day after."

"Anything new?"

"Yes! Mom's coming home to help us finish and tell the movers what goes where inside the truck. She'll get here Tuesday. I can't wait to see her. She's been gone three whole weeks!"

"Call tomorrow if you can," I say.

"I will. We're dropping those boxes off—the ones your folks said I could put in the basement. So I'll probably get to say hi then."

"Good."

We value the time that we have left.

≡ ≡ ≡ ≡ ≡ ≡ ≡ ≡ ≡ ≡ ≡ ≡ ≡

I come bursting out of the dream as if the demons who were chasing me all night are plunging toward the real world right behind me. I yell and grab my pillow like a shield. Then, out of the corner of my eye, I see a leg. It's white and small. Jerry's sitting beside me on the bed.

"Did you have a nightmare, Charlie?" He pulls back the curtain. A river of sunlight comes streaming through. I'm still clutching my pillow, but the fear is ebbing now. The birds are singing, like they do before it gets so hot.

"Mom could rock you in the rocking chair."

"Jerry, I'm thirteen years old! I don't need to be rocked."

"You were shouting and shouting."

"What did I say?"

"The words all ran together."

"Oh, well. It's daylight now, and I'm awake."

"Maybe we can go see Jess today."

= = = = = = = = = = = = = = =

I don't recall whether we do or not. The day passes quietly. I listen to music and watch a video. I think it rains sometime that afternoon. Later I see the boxes piled beside the furnace, and I know Shan must have come, even though I don't remember it. That memory is lost, like the next weeks—even months—are lost. Next thing I know, it's night again. I'm lying in my bed.

"I hear sirens," Jerry says.

I'm sound asleep, thinking his voice is in my dream. It's dark and peaceful where I am.

"Charlie."

He touches my arm.

"Charlie, I hear sirens. . . ."

= = = = = = = = = = = = = = =

I move out of the fog of sleep. Sirens are common for us. They're on the boulevard every night. We don't know if they're police or ambulance or fire trucks.

"What is it, Jerry?"

"They're loud." He pulls the curtain back again; it's dark outside. His voice changes. "Charlie, there's a house on fire."

"Here?"

He pulls it all the way back. I get out of bed, look out the window, and start screaming. I grab a pair of pants and pull them over my nightgown. "You stay here!" I yell at Jerry.

"I WON'T!"

"You have to. Go wake up Mom and Dad."

"NO."

I open their door myself. They're just dark lumps under the sheets. Their air conditioner's running, so they haven't heard a thing. I shove Jerry forward. "Wake them up." Then I go running down the stairs and out into the street.

= = = = = = = = = = = = = =

The front of Shan's house is in flames. There are three fire trucks parked beyond it, spraying water. The firemen are trying to put up ladders to the side and rear. The fire is so hot I can feel it blasting all the way over here, in my yard. The police have made a barrier. There are a few people inside it, but most neighbors are gathered on the sidewalk on my side of the street. "My God, my God," someone's crying. Another siren screams around the corner. It's an ambulance. The red light on top flicks on and off, on and off, like a clock measuring time.

= = = = = = = = = = = = = = =

"Charlie." It's Ms. Essie. She puts her arms around me. She's wearing a housecoat, and she doesn't even have her glasses on.

"Are they okay? What happened?"

"I don't know anything," she says.

"Did the sirens wake you up?"

"No, I heard an explosion. I looked outside, saw the fire, and called 911. They came right away."

"You didn't see Shan or her dad?"

She hugs my shoulder. "That doesn't mean anything, Charlie. They may be over there with the police."

= = = = = = = = = = = = = = =

But I don't see them. My folks come now, Dad holding Jerry in his arms like a baby. "Essie, what's—"

She cuts Dad off. "I don't know, Dom."

"Have the firemen been inside?"

"I think they're going to break the upstairs windows to get in."

"I don't see flames back there," I say. Then I realize that the stairs come down toward the front door, so that exit might be blocked. "Shan could jump from her window. It's not that far to the ground."

"You and Jerry need to go inside."

Without saying anything, I turn and hit Dad in the chest

with all my strength. His head snaps back, then he grabs my arm. I keep trying to hit him. He hugs me tight and doesn't let me go.

‗ ‗ ‗ ‗ ‗ ‗ ‗ ‗ ‗ ‗ ‗ ‗ ‗ ‗

Mom takes Jerry in, but Dad and I are still outside, in our front yard, when they bring the bodies out. Both of them are covered with sheets. I don't know which one is Shan's. The air stinks like wet ashes. Bobo doesn't like the sound of sirens, and he howls inside his pen. My dad picks me up and carries me inside, like I'm five years old and Shan and I were playing and I scraped my knee.

Thirty-six

Jerry and I sit on the front porch. All around us are green fields with cows in them. It's so quiet here: every now and then the sputter of a tractor, or a rooster crowing, or the cows crying when they want to come in to be milked. Early this morning, while I sat alone at Aunt Ellen's kitchen table, a deer and her baby came out of the woods and began to eat the apples under the apple tree in the front yard.

We've been here almost a month. School has started for the other kids. Twice a day we see the big old cheesebus rolling by. Pale faces stare at us from the windows. I don't smile or wave, because I'm not from here, and this isn't where I live.

= = = = = = = = = = = = = =

Aunt Ellen mailed the letter Jerry wrote to Jim using Jim's mother's address. Last week he got a letter back.

Dear Jerry,

I do not like the hospital in Port Arthur, Texas. They give me pills to stop me being crazy, mostly because they don't like it when I tell them about the future of this world, and the one to come.

It's sad about Shannon and her father. The devil works in strange ways: He takes the best—like Mr. Healy. But justice will come, because of you and what you did.

They took away my raincoat. My mother put it in the closet in the hall. Without it, I really can't remember who I am.

Jim

After I read it, I ripped the letter into a thousand pieces. Jerry was mad at me and cried and cried.

= = = = = = = = = = = = = =

They figured out how the fire got started. Two men poured gasoline around the outside of Shan's house. They tossed firebombs through the front and back windows. Then they lit the gas. They did it to keep Junie from coming back to be a witness at the trial.

My folks told Jerry, "We don't know how the fire got started." I think they're wrong to lie to him. Maybe that's why he believed the raincoat man; because the world they pretended for him after Mr. Healy died wasn't true. They say he's too young to know such awful things. I think that everyone should know that life can be this terrible.

= = = = = = = = = = = = = =

After I tore up the letter from the raincoat man, Jerry disappeared back into his own world: cars and bugs and animals. Aunt Ellen has two dogs, Beau and Fred, and the barn is full of cats, some of them wilder than the ones at the Exxon. Jerry hangs out with them. He'll take a book down to the barn and stay there all day long. Sometimes he lies in the yard and builds houses out of sticks and grass. Once he built a neighborhood, with twigs outlining yards and streets and alleys around the buildings. That night a storm blew in and knocked the whole thing down. But Jerry started another one beside the well house. He even dug a little lake, which he lined with plastic, so the water would stay inside. Sometimes he'll stick insects or caterpillars in his town. Then he'll pretend they're going to work or to the strip to buy ice cream.

But every night, Jerry cries. Sometimes he starts before he even gets tucked in. Other nights he'll drift off for a while and wake up screaming. Even when the light's turned on, he can't stop himself. It's not like he had a bad dream; he says he doesn't even know what makes him start. Aunt

Ellen lies beside him on the bed or sits and holds him on her lap. Sometimes when he's crying, I pull the covers over my head and talk to Mr. Healy. *I tried to watch out,* I whisper. *I didn't realize what was going on.* . . . Now and then I think I hear him say my name. His soft old voice is comforting. Then Jerry starts yelling in the other room, and I put my fingers in my ears and try to fall asleep. Sometimes he and Aunt Ellen are awake the whole night long.

= = = = = = = = = = = = = =

I think about Shan all the time. When I'm sitting on the porch here or by the stream that runs through Aunt Ellen's back field, or lying in bed staring at the blue-flowered wallpaper, what I really see is Shan. I see her sitting across from me in the Laundromat or eating french fries at McDonald's. I see her sitting cross-legged on Mr. Healy's porch, listening to stories. I see her putting on that silly little ring I traded for the bracelet her grandmother gave her. The last time I saw her, she was wearing it. I wonder how she felt before she died. Did she understand what happened? Did she think of me or Ray or Junie or her mom and dad? Did she know that she was going to die?

Whatever she thought or felt, whatever her body looked like on that stretcher, that was me, too. I'm burned and ugly now, but it's inside instead of out. There are blank spaces in my life that didn't used to be there: God and my block and my best friend, the rules that people live by and the reasons why they live at all. Maybe I'm like the raincoat man—with Shan killed, I really can't remember who I am.

= = = = = = = = = = = = = =

Shan's mom and Junie are in Chicago. We don't know if they're ever coming back. My folks say if they don't plan a memorial service here, we'll do one ourselves. I told them Shan was an atheist; she wouldn't want prayers or talk about heaven. At first they didn't believe me, but I said it over and over, until finally they did. The idea of a memorial service without prayers is hard for them to understand. But I know Shan better than anyone else here. Even if it makes other people uncomfortable, she deserves to be thought of and talked about as she really was.

= = = = = = = = = = = = = =

After the fire, my folks wouldn't let Jerry and me stay in the house by ourselves. They drove us here, to Fawn Grove, Pennsylvania, where Aunt Ellen lives. I was so numb I didn't argue. Jerry thought it was our vacation. We don't know when we're going back.

= = = = = = = = = = = = = =

Mom says there're changes in the neighborhood. Shan's house is being rebuilt, and a young couple signed a contract for Mr. Healy's. The man is a history teacher at Western High, and his wife makes pottery. She's going to have a studio on the first floor. Mom doesn't know if they were told what happened in the house or across the street at Shan's. She and Dad have almost finished the goldfish pond and the patio. They're waiting for Jerry and me to go with them to choose the fountain.

The city government's made changes, too. They have police on all the corners, even on the ones that were okay, and in the alley behind the shopping strip. The mayor drops by to visit every week. They had that meeting that was supposed to happen. People came from almost every house. They formed a foot patrol and a block watch and drew up a list of numbers so that neighbors could call each other if they needed to. Marcus and his aunt came, but she didn't say anything. Maybe she was tired of fooling herself about who her son turned out to be.

= = = = = = = = = = = = = =

I've gotten letters from kids at school and Ms. Essie and even Mr. Louras at the Laundromat. The best one came from Tuyen. She told it to Mr. M. in French, and he translated it because her English is so bad. Maybe he wrote it down while they were sitting in those chairs next to the swan fountain, with the smell of flowers all around.

She said that when she was a little child, her own

country—Vietnam—was torn apart by war. Houses were burned, and poison gases put into the air. Families had to live in tunnels underground. When the war ended and they came out from their hiding places, lots of their friends were dead, and everything they saw was ruined. Tuyen's family sent her and her brother away to France to live with strangers because there wasn't enough food or money or places to live in their own country.

> But the people who were left remembered what it had been like—the peach trees, the temples, and the rice fields—and they worked to build it back. It has taken a long, long time. But last year, for the first time in many years, I went home. My parents' house had been rebuilt, not in American style, but like it was before the war. People hugged me and said that they were glad that I was home. They gave me special food and sang old songs to welcome me. The life I left behind for all those years—the life I thought was lost—was there for me. Maybe it will be that way for you.

I read that letter to my dad. When I finished, there was silence on the other end of the line, so much quiet that I thought maybe we'd been cut off. When Dad finally spoke, I could tell that he'd been crying.

"Your room here, Charlie—that was my room, too, when I was little. Frankie and Joe had bunks in Jerry's room."

I know, I know. . . .

"Pop worked too hard, and he was always mad when he got home. We got the belt too much. But outside, we had people to look out for us, places to go if we were hungry or got hurt or needed something that we couldn't get at home. When I was in Iraq, hearing the shells go off and scared out of my mind, you know what I thought about?"

I wait.

"I thought about the neighborhood. To calm myself, I walked through every single yard, up the steps, into the kitchens, where they'd give me milk or braciola or bread and butter. I remembered how glad they seemed to see me. I said their names over and over so I could fall asleep: Cantelli, Lupa, Velli, Brill, Howard, Biagi—that was the house Ms. Essie bought. All those nights, I dreamed of one thing: home. When you and Jerry came along, I was so happy that we lived here, in this place. Maybe I didn't want to see how things had changed.

"But now I do. And I know how to fight, and I'm strong, and I won't give up."

"You're only one person."

"That's true. But if I have to, I'll stand on that corner every single day."

= = = = = = = = = = = = = =

In my mind I see Dad on the corner. He's bolt upright, like a soldier, his arms across his chest. I remember his voice that time he spoke to Jim, how certain it was, like what he said was law. He and I fight because he'll never, ever give in. But now that he's decided there won't be drugs on Lanvale Street, he'll take on challengers. You'd be crazy to want to fight my dad. With the police around to back him up, the gangs may move away, where no one cares. And maybe the other neighbors can stand behind him without feeling so afraid.

= = = = = = = = = = = = = =

"When can we come home?" I ask.

"Not yet."

= = = = = = = = = = = = = =

But it's been weeks. Every day I look out my bedroom window at the green fields that Jess's songs made me imagine, and I see that beauty is nothing without the people you care about. I miss so many of them, even Mr. Tibby, with his torn-up shoe. When I try to describe him to Aunt Ellen, she gets this funny look, like it's hard for her to understand how a worn-out crackhead could be part of anybody's dreams.

= = = = = = = = = = = = = =

Jerry's doing better than he was when we first came. Sometimes he misses Mom and Dad a lot and cries for Bobo. Other times he's pretty normal—and annoying, like he used to be. This morning at breakfast he was getting on my nerves. "Charlie, you have to see this. It's the best!"

"What?"

"It's a surprise."

"I don't want to be surprised."

"Yes you do. You just don't know it yet." He takes my hand and drags me to the stream behind the house. He's still wearing his pajamas, with no shoes, and before I can say anything, he wades into a shallow pool. The water makes a lovely soft sound running over the stones and sand. The stream sparkles in the sunlight, except the spot where Jerry's stirred up dust. I don't want to be here, and I start to walk back to the house.

"Just a minute more, Charlie. You have to see this." He stands there, hands on his skinny hips, with this big grin across his face. As the water clears, he points straight down. It takes me a minute to see what he's pointing at: There are little silver minnows swarming around his feet. Each time he moves, they follow him. I look at him and he's so happy, like nothing in his life will ever be better than this. For an instant I feel a spark of light inside myself. It's sharp, like pain. Before I realize what's happened, it has disappeared.

"Charlie, take off your shoes!"

"I don't want to."

"You should!"

I shake my head and sit down on the bank to wait for him.